PRINCE OF

GLUTTONY

PRINCES OF SIN:
SEVEN DEADLY SINS SERIES

K. ELLE MORRISON

This novel is a work of fiction. All characters and events portrayed are products of author's imagination and used fictitiously.
Editing by Caroline Acebo
Proofreading by Norma's Nook Proofreading
Cover Designed by Cassie Chapman at Opulent Designs
Interior page design by K. Elle Morrison

Kellemorrison.com

Print ISBN: 9798867731786
Ebook ISBN: 979-8-9887063-5-9

To Ash
For so much

DEAR READERS

This book contains material that may be considered inappropriate for readers under the age of 18.

These materials cover:
Graphic sex between consenting adults, BDSM, mental health crisis, drug and alcohol abuse, and pegging. Please be aware that there may be elements of religious trauma.

Please leave a review ;)

OTHER TITLES BY K. ELLE MORRISON

To stay up-to-date on upcoming titles, bonus material, advanced reader opportunities, and so much more visit Kellemorrison.com to join the newsletter!

For all upcoming projects and updates from K. Elle Morrison please subscribe to the _FREE_ Newsletter!

Kellemorrison.com
Linktree

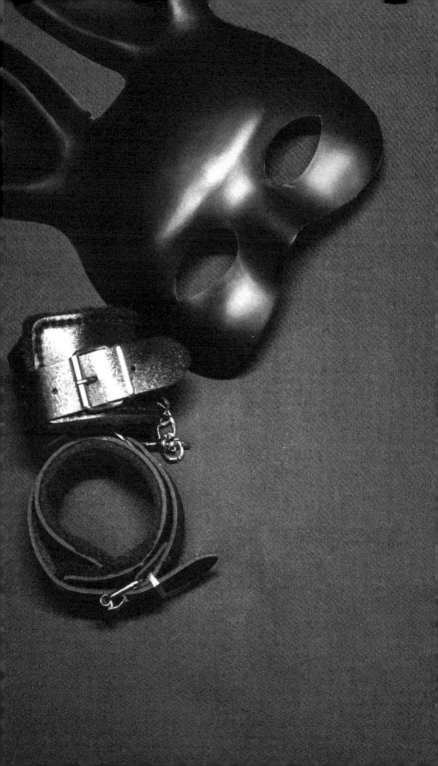

CHAPTER 1
OROBAS

I had it all. But I needed more.

Two pairs of eyes stared greedily up at me. The humans slid their lips over each side of my shaft, competing to stretch theirs over the tip. My cock was the barrier to tongues and teeth.

Music piped from the strip club into the private room did little to mask the sounds of sucking, fucking, and strained voices toeing the line of pleasure and ruin.

Fevered bodies covered the floor. Hips and heads swayed in the lust-dense air. Sex, spit, and desperation fueled me.

A third human crawled from the throng to join the other two. I laid my head back on the pillow and gladly let my face become her throne, where she could rule over the frenzy.

Her pussy was still hot from previous usage, but I lapped at it until her thighs trembled around my temples.

Her fingers in my hair held me still so she could grind her clit against my lips and the tip of my nose.

Someone claimed my cock with a hole and bounced wildly on it out of sight.

I was blessed with a cock worth its length and girth in gold. My vessel was made for use, and I relished every inch of my own skin. My gift for unquenchable thirst brought humans to their knees in the hope that my cum would coat their taste buds and fill their souls with the satisfaction they craved.

But I was death by overstimulation. My touch left humans crazed with hunger. Inspired all reason to abandon them. My body had been the end of many lives, and I'd loved every moment of it.

My palm smacked the ass bouncing on my chin, and the owner let out a shriek before sliding down my torso and into the lap of the human still riding my cock. She tasted herself on my lips and whimpered for more.

"Water," I demanded, and she rose with a disappointed groan.

Her face was quickly replaced by a set of glitter-dusted breasts that I promptly tongued.

Unlike my kin, never once had I regretted my choice to Fall. I belonged among the deviants. I had willingly squandered my potential in Heaven to writhe with mortals and the damned. I'd known only pleasure and freedom since.

The Prince of Greed and the Prince of Lust sat in the cushioned booths around the scene, joined by Ezequiel, a Watcher Angel. Stolas and I came as a pair more often than not, but our invite by Sitri was a rare occasion. If it hadn't been for his recent attempt at curing his loneliness, I would have departed from the group hours ago to find my own trouble. But as it was, he was enjoying the delirium I was causing. A benefit I bestowed with mirth.

I looked over at my most eloquent brother, Stolas, who was scrolling through his phone and refusing to unleash his cock for the greedy humans at his feet. He gave a sigh. "Are you finished with your puppets?"

I lifted my face from the dancer's soft flesh and laughed. "If you strain any tighter, that stick up your ass is going to manifest itself into a diamond just so you grant it mercy and retrieve it."

Stolas rolled his eyes and put his phone away. "You have ten minutes to play before our appointment." He stood and brushed the wrinkles from his tailored suit. "I'll be waiting outside. Don't make a mess, Oro."

He knew exactly what to say to bring my most savage urges to the surface. Ezequiel joined him, leaving me and the Prince of Lust alone to have our way with the six dancers.

The Watcher said something to Sitri as he left but I was too enthralled to listen too carefully. When the two fuddy-duddies exited, I watched as Sitri pulled a rather impressive cock from a dancer's tight briefs and took it deep into his throat. The prince bobbed faster as his hands explored the man's round, taut ass cheeks. His fingers circled the man's tight hole until he'd wiggled inside and the dancer begged for more.

"Don't be such a tease, Prince of Lust," I cooed,

twisting the nipples of the woman perched on my lap as she circled her cunt on my cock.

Sitri hadn't taken his cock out at any of the clubs we'd hit before this one. I hadn't felt the familiar brush of his influence converge with mine or Stolas' either. Where there had always been wild beasts banging on the gates that withheld his power, there were now sleeping kittens.

It was infuriating because there was nothing I could do to force him to admit he had been broken by a woman and a lowly duke. The rumors of his abilities being stripped were already too much on their own, but witnessing his depleted potential had been sickening.

I took hold of the wispy hip bones on my groin. The woman yelped when I dug my nails into her, then grunted wildly as I relentlessly brought her down on my cock. Her ass slapped my thighs until the head of my climax filled her. My seed spilled over and covered my lower stomach when I tossed her to the side. Her cunt was replaced by two mouths licking me clean.

The dancer I'd just fucked lay on her back on the floor, dipping her fingers into her pussy and then bringing them to her mouth like my fluid was golden honey. She whined when a mouth sucked over her cunt to steal the last taste of me from her folds.

I huffed a laugh through my nose at the scene. Out of the corner of my eye, I saw Sitri get to his feet. He spat something to the ground—I assumed the release of the man he'd been pleasuring—and picked up a bottle of champagne. He took a long swig then handed it to one of the dancers.

The crowded main floor was a frenzy of bodies feeling the residual threads of my manic power. The men who lined the stage pounded their red fists on the polished platform as one woman straddled the face of another. A plexiglass wall separated the animals from the spectacle they desperately wanted.

Disgusting desperation took hold of them as each began to go rabid with their desires. They clawed and tore at the nearest flesh and foamed at the mouth until screams of frustration turned to pain, then to the wheeze of exhaustion, and finally the rattle of death.

We reached the main exit and I glanced back to a bloodbath. The dancers started to come to and wordlessly mouthed questions of shock. The creeping smile on my lips made Sitri roll his eyes and gesture to the door.

"Ready to go?" Sitri asked, shaking out the lapels of his jacket.

"Onward into the night, for she is balmy and full of delights." I smiled and got to my feet to follow him out.

Out on the sidewalk, Stolas and Ezequiel eyed us.

"Two minutes to spare. A new record, dear brother," Stolas said with a mocking clap of his hands.

I put my crisp white shirt over my battered body. "In my defense, I left a few intact."

Sitri grinned and masked what we'd inflicted with a passive chuckle. "Finally learning some discipline. And they say you can't teach an old demon new tricks."

With our departure, screams of madness rang out as witnesses to the massacre rushed in. My influence had waned, and clarity seeped into the broken minds left in our wake. The streets of Sin City were ripe with souls and holes for owning, and I was only made hungrier with each one I devoured. It was too easy to line our pockets with the souls of the fools who gambled and fucked about the streets.

CHAPTER 2
AMBER

My whip over the sub's ass snapped through the air, electrifying the damp heat, and sent a shiver up his spine. His muffled moan through the ball gag fed the low tension mounting in my stomach.

He was a regular to the BDSM nights at The Deacon but wouldn't commit to a full-time position. Whatever he did for work kept him from his truest desires most days of the month.

"Are you ready to be a good boy, Allen?" I ran a gloved finger down his slick spine.

He whimpered and shook.

"Louder, puppy," I demanded with a smack of the crop on the other cheek.

"Mmm," he agreed as best he could.

I walked over to the single chair in the hidden room and sat with my legs wide open. His eyes went straight to my pussy, and his pupils blew to three times their normal size. He picked up his hand from the floor and made to remove the gag from his mouth.

"Not yet," I said, slapping the riding crop into my open palm. "Crawl to me. On your belly."

He immediately obeyed, getting flat on the floor and pulling himself across it.

His fingers reached my boots and wrapped around my ankles. But like the good boy he was, he stopped and waited for permission. I loved it when a sub knew his place. I gave him a short nod, and he removed the gag gingerly from between his swollen lips. He'd been stretched for over an hour, and the dry skin was irritated and likely sore.

Good. He'd have something to remember me by the next day.

His tongue lazed out and ran up the fine leather of my boots to my knee, then over my thigh. But when he got to my center, he stopped once more and waited.

"Do you want it?" I kept my tone low and calm, but inside I was ready to burst.

He nodded. "Please, Mistress."

Mistress. The name grated my nerves. Allen wasn't the most imaginative of accountants, so when we set up our arrangement, he hadn't thought of a name that suited me better.

"Beg," I said sternly.

"Just a taste. I need just one taste, please." He licked his lips, inching closer to my pulsing center.

I placed one finger on the middle of his forehead and

stopped him just far enough away so that his tongue couldn't reach my clit.

"I want to suck your pretty clit, please. I'll do anything for a taste." His voice got more desperate with every new word, but he didn't push against the pressure of my finger.

"Please, Mistress. Oh please." His groveling finally won him the prize.

I removed my hand and shifted my ass forward to his face. He gave me one last glance before diving into my cunt, his tongue and lips wildly working my nerves. I bit down on my lip, holding back the mounting orgasm a little longer to savor the time we'd spent because once I'd had my fill, he would be permitted to be relieved and our session would be finished.

The sounds of his mouth over my cunt mixed with his wanton mewls, edging me closer to the pinnacle of my release. I placed my hand on the back of his head to hold him still as I circled my wetness over his lips and outstretched tongue.

"Such a good boy for me. Did you earn this pussy as a treat?"

Incoherent whines punctuated his fervent lapping. His hands spread me open, and his thumbs worked over my entrance as his tongue greedily kneaded my clit. I was so close but needed more. I held him firm and ground against his nose, stealing his oxygen.

"That's it, puppy. You only breathe to make me come," I gritted out through clenched teeth.

Two of his fingers slipped inside my pussy and massaged just the right spot. I pulsed and moaned and cursed as I rode his face through my orgasm. I loosened my grip and let him suck in a lungful of air, but gifted him the pleasure of slow swipes of his tongue over my throbbing cunt until the aftershocks receded.

My body relaxed and the afterglow settled into my bones. Allen laid his head on my thigh and glued his eyes to my wet heat while he stroked himself furiously. Only a moment later, his body tensed and shuddered with his release.

He sighed and laid a kiss on my clit before looking up at me, his role as sub quickly slipping away as our scene ended and real life came rushing back.

"Thank you, Amber. Fuck." He heaved another sigh and got to work cleaning up our mess.

The demon prince who owned the club hated a dirty room, and it was Allen's job to ensure my place in Sitri's good graces remained intact.

"You had the walls shaking tonight, Amber," Sitri teased from the other side of the bar.

It was well past closing time, and he was helping the bartender clean up. I liked Sitri. He was handsome, smart, and knew when to respect boundaries. We had slept together years ago, but our natures didn't connect. I was too domineering for his taste, and he was too much of a flirt for mine. When he offered me a place to run my BDSM night with a close-knit group of celebrity friends, I knew our lives would be tangled for a long time, which meant we had to trust each other.

Trust, after all, was the foundation of any relationship. It was what everyone in our community strived for. I trusted Allen to be discreet, on time, and bring me pleasure. He trusted me with his secrets, dignity, and deepest desires.

"It was thrilling and you know it." Ezequiel scoffed from his usual perch at the end of the bar. He rarely went anywhere without Sitri in sight.

"You two are worse than two old hens." I smirked and sat on the stool facing Sitri.

"We rely on you to liven up the place." Ezequiel returned my sass with a dazzling smile. "Otherwise, it's just the B-list celebrities and newbie influencers on Wednesday nights."

"Bite your tongue," Sitri snapped playfully. "Three of those influencers sold me their souls tonight and booked an event next week with all their followers in the tri-county area."

Ezequiel rolled his eyes and ran his tongue along his too-white teeth; I wondered who he'd sunk those pearly bits into earlier.

I'd never let them take me to bed together, though they'd offered the first night we met. One heavenly rejected being penetrating me at a time was plenty. I wasn't positive about what Ezequiel was. They called him Watcher or angel or a traitor. All those titles could have been true, but he never let me close enough to find out for myself. His tarnished demeanor and radiant personality often clashed with his mannerisms and behaviors.

He *was* a bit funny about humans. If he liked them, he didn't touch them. If he was indifferent, he fucked them silly. I suspected it was his way of defending the bruised heart he'd harbored for his whole existence. Who knew an ancient being would be so easily seen through?

Sitri poured me a vodka soda, squeezed a lime over it, then dropped the wedge onto the ice, just how I liked it.

"How was Vegas?" I asked.

My question perked their brows. Though neither verbally answered, an unspoken word passed between them.

I took a long sip from my glass, but the silent seconds that went by were awkward. "Oh, come on, you two. Usually, I can't get either one of you to shut up after you skip off to Sin City for the weekend. What gives?"

"Sitri and I have a new . . . employee." Ezequiel blushed, and I mean he really *blushed*. "She started the night we got back from Las Vegas."

"Yeah, okay. Did you find them in Vegas?" Getting a straight answer from a demon was always harder than pulling teeth with a butter knife.

"No," Sitri said too quickly. "We were chosen to foster their exploration of this plane."

"Oh fuck no." I raised my hands as if the bartop were suddenly on fire. "What did you release on Earth this time?"

I vividly remembered the time someone let an incubus loose in the club. It had taken hours and three EMTs to revive the poor humans who'd succumbed to its power on the dance floor. The nightmare with the police department meant that my group hadn't been able to perform for two weeks following the incident.

"It's not like that," Ezequiel assured me and slid my drink closer. "She's a true neutral being."

"A true neutral? So she's not an angel or a demon?"

"She's a Reaper," Sitri said. His low tone felt defensive. "She won't be here long, but don't be surprised if you run into her. She'll be working the bar until her time is up."

"That's not ominous at all," I snarked and bottomed up my glass to suck the liquor down as fast as I could, hoping to chase away the memory of this conversation.

Sometimes, I hated knowing what I did. Being able to see these powerful beings for what they truly were made me realize how thin the veil holding back a lot of messy family history was. Believing in some sort of divine master plan after knowing demons for so long seemed foolish, but it gave me all the more reason to live as freely as possible.

"We felt it was only fair to warn you." Ezequiel raised a glass of something amber and thick then downed it without a wince.

"I appreciate it." I tapped the side of my glass, feeling the effects starting to settle into my sore muscles. "I'm off. See you boys tomorrow night."

They gave courteous salutes and went back to closing up the bar for the night. I took my things from my locker at the door, and the lesser spirit acting as bouncer walked me out like a good little minion of the damned to the car I had called.

After safely sliding into the back seat of the vehicle, I pulled out my phone and read the first text:

SIMONS

$500 for one night on my arm.

I rolled my eyes at the corporate lawyer's message.

AMBER

That's only half my rate.

SIMONS

I want to show you off on Friday night.

Just a party with many men who will not be able to take their eyes off you and their wives, who will be insanely jealous of your beauty.

AMBER

$800

SIMONS

$900

AMBER

You're terrible at haggling. $1000

SIMONS

I want you to wear a new dress.

AMBER

In that case, $2000

SIMONS

Something tight and red. You know how much I love the color red on you.

> **AMBER**
>
> $2500

> **SIMONS**
>
> You're making me so hard, baby. I miss you. $3000

> **AMBER**
>
> If you really missed me, you'd be on your knees on my doorstep.

> **SIMONS**
>
> $4000 and I'll save my knees for a stolen moment during the party.

> **AMBER**
>
> Send me the details.

> **SIMONS**
>
> Send me one photo.

A notification from my bank flashed at the top of my phone, alerting me that Simons had deposited $5000 into my account. I took a quick photo of my hand cupping my breast over my white silk shirt. The flash of my phone showed the swell of my cleavage and my black bra through the thin material.

He sent back an emoji with a red face sweating and panting, then the details of the party.

> **SIMONS**
>
> I'll pick you up at 6pm Friday. It's at the senator's mansion. I can't wait to see you. XO

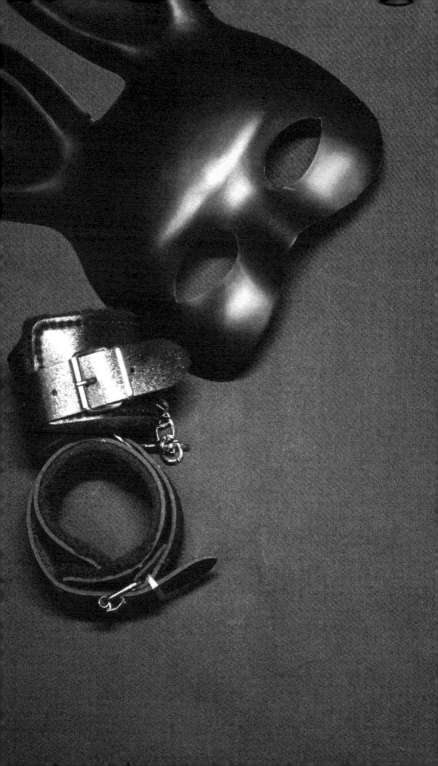

CHAPTER 3
OROBAS

Friday night, I owed Stolas an introduction to the soul I'd lost to him during a round of poker with him and Sitri. I should have known not to mix molly with tequila. By a twist of fate, my longest con was the only soul I had worth betting. I likely could have made an even trade with Stolas, but what was the fun in that?

When we entered the Gerhardt mansion, it was buzzing with wrinkled politicians, socialites, and old money. Women hung on their much-older sugar daddies as they clucked to one another about which vineyard they were summering at. It was always the same show of hubris at events like these, but each pair was prime for the picking.

Stolas pulled on my elbow, reeling me in as I absent-mindedly veered toward a particularly gaudy couple who were dressed far too formally. "Not yet. You'll get your time to roam after I'm satisfied with my winnings."

"Dearest and most esurient brother, I would never

want to satisfy you. Then who would I play with?" I gave him a wink and moved us through the crowd toward Evelyn Gerhardt. "Evie, there you are. I was just looking for your father."

I allowed my eyes to wander over what was no longer mine one last time.

"Oro, good evening," she answered and peered through the crowd for her father. "I just saw him with the CEO of Solar Star."

Unless the CEO of the solar company was interested in a threesome with Harris and his young wife, I doubted very much that Evie had seen them together.

"I'm sure he'll find us in a moment. Busy man, your father." I exchanged a knowing smirk with Stolas then turned back to Evie to introduce them. "This is my brother and business partner. I don't believe you've had the plea-sure of meeting the senator's daughter Evie."

Her eyes on my brother dilated to the point where I couldn't remember the color of her irises. She'd never looked at me that way, and it stung my ego just a little.

"It's nice to meet you . . . ," she started.

"Stolas." My brother's true name left his lips, and my ears perked at the willingness.

"Stolas," she repeated carefully. "That's a . . . strong name."

"Suits him, doesn't it?" I clapped his shoulder and beamed with pride. "Handsome devil. My glass is empty, bad luck at such a fancy affair. I'll be back in a moment."

I moved away as she shook herself from her stupor. Like a moth to a flame, she was under Stolas' spell already, and who was I to break up what was sure to be the start to a most filmic tragedy?

"Oh, I can—" She tried to free herself from his invisible clutches, but the poor dear was already too deep.

"No, please stay and occupy my brother. He has been bored to tears and I need a rest from carrying the conversation for the both of us." I slipped between two passing bodies and out of sight.

My eyes swept the room before I ascended the staircase in search of the most expensive booze hidden away in Harris' study liquor cabinet. The last time I'd come to the Gerhardt home, I'd eyed a bottle of Macallan M that he'd been saving for a special occasion. Perhaps me handing his daughter's soul off to my brother was special enough.

At the top of the stairs was a woman looking over the banister at the party below. Every bit of her caught my eye, from the curves of her hips and breasts, hugged by a flawless deep red dress, to her long hair that sat high on the crown of her head and cascaded down her back. Even the bored, distracted expression on her face had my mouth watering.

Who was this goddess, and why wasn't I on my knees with my head between her legs?

I sidled up to her and leaned an arm on the banister to cage her into me. She glanced over, but that was the only acknowledgment she gave me.

"I'm going to go out on an olive branch here and say you're waiting for someone?" My fingers itched to caress her smooth, perfect skin but I'd surely catch fire if I did.

Her brow perked, but she still didn't turn her head.

The beast in my chest begged even louder for her full attention, even for a momentary askance.

"I am." She brought a champagne flute up to her ruby lips and took a short sip.

"And he dared leave you unattended with these rich vultures around?"

The only millionaire monster roaming these halls she had to worry about was the one breathing in her vanilla and spice perfume like it was the last bit of oxygen in a sinking submarine.

Finally, she faced me. Her eyes fixed on mine for a breath then scanned me before she spoke. "Do I look defenseless?"

I wanted to get on my hands and knees right then and there to kiss the hem of her dress. She was gorgeous, and the air she exuded was an intoxicating mixture of power and pure sex.

"Not if your tongue is as sharp as the daggers you're staring into me," I said, reeling myself in before I scared her off. "I'd wager your words could cut my ego deeper than most blades."

It was only the smallest of twitches, but the corner of her mouth lifted for a second and I caught my opening. I dared to trail a finger down the back of her arm. Goose bumps raised on her silky brown skin in my wake. Another brief crack in her iron exterior.

"I could be dimwitted and dull. You only care about what you see." Her gaze went back to the crowd below.

"I'll never know unless you permit me a moment of

your time to get to know what's inside that gorgeous head of yours."

"I don't allow demons in my head."

I internally recoiled. How could she possibly know what I was within moments of meeting me?

I looked down at the edge of the sigil on my wrist that peeked out from beneath my shirt cuff. To me, it was obvious, but most humans would assume demon sigils were nothing more than lame graffiti.

Unless she knew other demons well.

"How many demons cozied up to you before you became so acquainted that you could spot one at a party full of sinners?"

"Two." She took another sip and refused to look at me.

A voice in my head turned fanatic, losing all rationale. Clamoring for her brown eyes to consume me whole and leave nothing but crumbs. Another voice screamed for the throats of the demons who'd touched this perfect woman before I had a chance to sink my teeth into her. They were stupid enough to let her go. I would not make that mistake.

But before I could speak again, Harris fumbled from the guest bedroom behind us, his wife adjusting her lipstick close behind him. Their faces were flushed, their hair just slightly mussed.

"Ah, the man of the hour. Find a good lobbyist in there, Harris?" I teased, and his wife's peachy face went crimson.

"Oro." Harris' tone held a threat, but it was as weak as his stroke game.

"Becky." I grinned at her and fixed my eyes on the bit

of cleavage she hadn't put away just yet. "You look lovely as always."

A third human came out of the bedroom. The man locked his sight on the woman next to me, then on the couple he was just having a private interaction with.

"Amber, let's go back to the party," he said and offered his arm.

Harris and his wife started downstairs without another word. The woman, Amber, took the stranger's arm and turned her face up to him with a smile that made my core catch fire.

"Thank you for keeping an eye on my date," the human said to me as his arm snaked around her waist. He was closer to death than he realized. "Noble of you."

I watched as they descended the stairs, already planning how I would drink her memory away, when her eyes flashed up to mine. Our gazes held for two beats of my stone heart before her date's hand cupped her chin and brought her lips to his.

My blood boiled. The act was clearly meant to incite a war.

I watched the tops of their heads slip out of sight as they went deeper into the house. I gave it only a minute before I made my way down the steps after them. Stolas and Evelyn were nowhere to be seen, which was my preference. I didn't need Stolas to police whatever I chose to do when the moment arrived.

Amber's dark hair swung back and forth as she and her date walked through the living room and into the dining room toward the bar, which was being kept by a man who instantly lit up when he saw her. I added this nameless man to the growing list of humans I was willing to end for being given something I desperately craved.

"Oro, there you are," said an irritating voice that breached my concentration. "I thought I saw your brother a moment ago."

Greg was an accountant for the city who worked closely with Harris. He wrapped an arm around my shoulder and led me away. "Come, I want to introduce you to the head of Solar Star. Great contact to make at one of these functions. Networking, you know."

I searched the room for Amber, but I'd lost her.

"Yes, she just graduated." A tall man with salt-and-pepper hair was chatting with a small group that looked at him as if he'd not only harnessed the sun, but it shined out of his ass. "My sweet Prudence is going to come work for me in a few months, after she settles in at her new apartment. She really is my little angel."

"Thomas, this is Oro. He and his brother run the investment firm I was talking about," Greg said, nudging me closer to the pompous CEO.

"It's great to finally meet the magical Oro. Greg talks so highly of you, I was sure you were a myth."

"Many think I am." I smiled wide, turning on the charm that had won me souls and business agreements.

Thomas held out his hand then took mine when I obliged. It was a solid handshake, not weak or overpowering to compensate for any lack of status. When he pulled away, I got the impression that he'd heard my name before. He'd held my gaze for several moments too long to have been a stranger. Perhaps we had made a bargain in the past?

"What sort of investment portfolios are you working with, Oro?" Thomas pulled three cigars out of his pocket and offered one to me, then one to a man to his right.

"Are you looking to add to it?" I took the cigar and unwrapped it.

"Always." He held out a guillotine and a small matchbox. A glowing martini glass with an olive speared on a thin cross-shaped pick was printed on it.

It was a familiar image.

"You've been to The Deacon, then?" I held up the box and shook it before taking out a single red and black dyed match.

I struck it against the matte strike strip and took a puff from my cigar. We stood a moment in the silent challenge I'd presented.

He pursed his lips and gave a small shake of his head. "I must have gotten it from my daughter. I keep myself away from the riffraff."

I took a puff from my cigar and watched Thomas's brow twitch. "Smart."

That was where this man had had the pleasure of encountering me before this official introduction. Odd that he was guarding his reputation in the company of blasphemers.

Out of the corner of my eye, I saw Amber and her date. As much as I wanted to press the matter with Thomas the secretive CEO, I had more self-serving matters to attend to. Like winning the glory between Amber's legs.

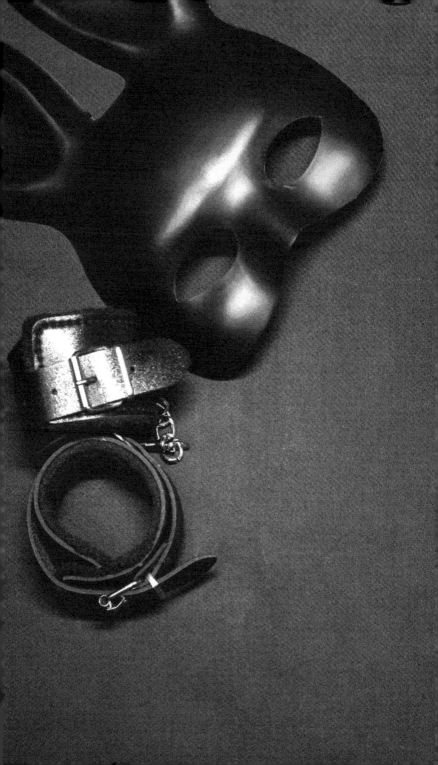

CHAPTER 4
AMBER

Simons was making the rounds one last time before he escorted me out. I'd given him plenty of reasons to take me somewhere more private, but knowing there was at least one demon present told me that the attending company was in more danger than they likely knew.

I made it a point to stay out of the affairs of the damned and the holy. Once one side had been revealed to me—by accident—the other had made their introductions via a lesser angel named Haziel. They had made themselves known after I'd made an agreement with the demon they constrained. Eligos was easy to talk to, and even easier to fall into bed with. Little did I know that his less common nickname was the Collector. Haziel deemed me worthy of a warning, but I hadn't listened. The deal I'd struck with Eligos garnered me an invitation to The Deacon and into the very small inner circle of humans who had the pleasure of *knowing*.

Whatever status of demon Oro was didn't matter. I knew by the way the air shifted around him that he was otherworldly. Not meant to be mixing so casually with humankind. It was similar to how my body reacted to Sitri and Ezequiel. Like something outside of myself was commanding my innards to answer an unheard call to attention.

That sensation washed over me for the second time that evening, causing the hair on the back of my neck to rise from a brush of his skin.

"Leaving so soon?" Oro whispered in my ear, his hot breath sinking into my core.

"Yes." I didn't turn around. Acknowledging a demon's interest was just feeding their ego.

"Where has your date run off to this time? Another clandestine threesome?"

"I wouldn't know."

"Pity." He moved in closer, and the warm scent of his cologne surrounded me.

"What part of me standing alone makes you think I want to have a conversation with you?" I let the irritation come through my words.

"You don't want me to admit what part of you wants to hear me talk."

Cocky asshole. "Settle down."

A throaty laugh vibrated in his chest, which was now pressed against my shoulder. "You said that like you demand obedience often."

I didn't answer.

"Have you ever been to The Deacon?" He pulled back, but his voice remained low and deep.

"Why?" My eyes snapped to his, and the mistake sent ice through my veins.

The curl of his lips was enough to melt off anyone's panties, but I wasn't wearing any. And his cheek made my palm itch.

"It's one of the most exclusive clubs in the city for a reason. The perfect place for someone like you."

He was being cryptic.

"Someone like me?"

"You know what I am and have the ability to refrain from any urges you may experience in my presence. It's a rare commodity, to say the most."

"Or you think very highly of yourself and overestimate your influence on this plane." The hit of my words landed on his ego.

"Meet me at The Deacon this weekend, and I'll change your mind."

I couldn't tell if he was being cocky—because he very well could break the barriers I'd practiced to refuse demonic influences—or if he was searching for a connection between me and the demon bar. I knew demons frequented the place, which was known for turning secret hopes into granted dreams. Those wishes came with a price, and the payment was undetectable until it was far too late.

"I'm busy." I broke my gaze away from his. I heard the intake of breath then felt his body stiffen.

"I'm not below begging on my knees in front of these

people. Grovel at your feet as they all watch with pity and horror on their faces."

I looked around the room and found several eyes on us, all women who looked as if they would kill to be exactly where I stood. They couldn't hear his offer, but he was as hot as the sins he inflicted.

"That spark in your eyes says you'd like to see me on all fours for you," he continued, putting more images in my head. "At your mercy."

My mouth watered. I knew what sort of power I could experience with a demon. Dominating a being of chaos and temptation was a high I'd never experienced before, but it likely would come with the lowest of lows and no amount of aftercare could soothe the withdrawal.

No. I had to say no.

"Tomorrow night. VIP floor." His fingers played through the ends of my hair. "Unless you'll grant me permission to show you how good of a boy I could be right here?"

I held my breath, waiting for the rush of lust to simmer. Simons glanced my way and gave me a tilt of his head, our subtle way of communicating in a crowded room.

Are you okay?

I held my hand up to my waist and gave him two gestures with my fingers. *I'm fine. Let's go.*

He looked back at the couple he'd been talking to and bid them farewell. When the code was made, it demanded an immediate response. He was making his way over before Oro made his next promise.

"Until we meet again, Miss Amber."

I knew he was gone before I turned to make sure, and not just from my side. He'd left the party altogether. As Sitri called it, he had stepped through a void and retreated to wherever dark and dangerous things hid from the world.

Simons tucked me in close to lead me out to his car. Once there, he opened the passenger-side door for me but caught my hand before I could get inside.

"Amber, are you okay?" His sweet voice felt like a cool dousing of water after being in an inferno.

I smiled and wound my fingers around his. "Nothing you couldn't fix with your tongue."

He blushed and eagerly ushered me to sit. He took me back to his place. Another woman might have felt guilty for taking her sexual frustrations out on another man's hide, but Simons lived for my crop. And he deserved a treat for his show of loyalty, after all.

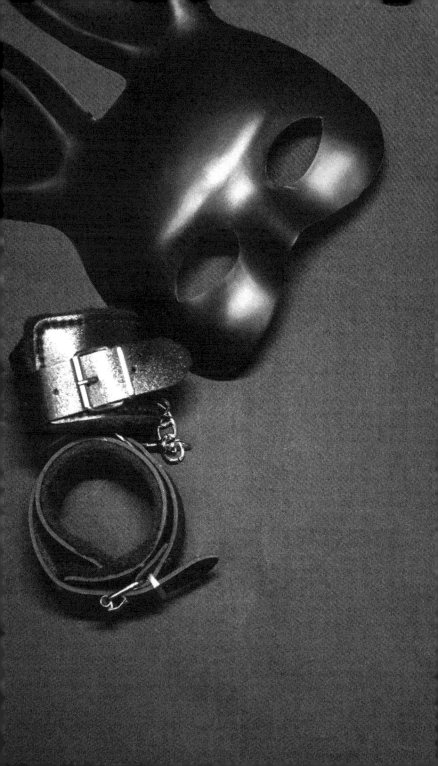

CHAPTER 5
OROBAS

To keep myself from searching the crowd for the mysterious mistress, I drank my way through two of my brother's top shelves and had started on a third by the time I'd found a bountiful bosom to suffocate in. She was splayed out on the table at the center of the VIP booth as I lapped up a scotch older than she was out of her belly button then trailed my mouth up her body.

I clutched her thigh with one hand, my thumb circling her clit as my tongue teased a taut nipple through her lace bra. Her thighs clenched as her climax overtook her, and she ignored Stolas when he plopped down next to me.

He looked as if he'd seen a ghost's ass while in the bathroom.

I cocked a brow at him over the swell of the woman's heaving breasts. "What's the matter with you?"

"Nothing," he grumped.

"That's convincing." I filled two glasses and took a

shot. "You have a scowl on your face that could scare the paint off a bus."

He scowled at the moisture on my fingers when I offered him the other shot glass. "You might want to slow down. It's not even midnight and you've lost your senses."

My distraction got up from the table and adjusted her skirt, though there wasn't much fabric to cover the swollen pussy I'd just been pleasuring. Like a smitten puppy, she found a spot to perch and linger.

"And besmirch my title? Brother, some of us cannot rely on our attitudes to spread our gifts to the masses. I am excess. All revelry and misguided fun must be inspired by my hand." My arms flung out. "I am all of this."

"Calm down, brother." Ezequiel's voice interrupted my declaration.

The angelic tart came to sit with a beautiful woman cuddled into him. "Hope you don't mind if we join you," he stated.

"It depends," I answered. "Did you bring anything for the rest of us?"

"Oro," Sitri warned as he came through the crowd. "You'll behave around our guests." He allowed several others to file into the booth, and the last brought a cocky smile to my drunken face.

"Evie!" I called.

Her eyes darted between Stolas and me, as they should. What were the odds she would run into us here?

Sitri wrapped his arm around Evie's shoulder and brought her to his side. I stole a glance at Stolas. His ears were flushed. I waited in pure rapture for the possibility of a fight over a human.

"You didn't say you knew my brother?" Sitri said into Evie's temple.

"I didn't know Oro and Stolas were your brothers," she answered, her voice careful.

"A lovely surprise all around, it would seem." Ezequiel had noticed the shift in the air too. He smiled with amusement while he watched Stolas contemplate his next move.

"Wait, Evie. Isn't this the guy you were talking to downstairs?" one of Evie's friends remarked as they settled in.

"I say that calls for a toast." I signaled to the waitress, and she promptly bustled to work.

"This has just turned into a much more interesting night than I had foreseen," Sitri mused.

Each person wore a completely different expression. From lust-filled eyes to confusion to utter bewilderment, not one emotion circling us was cohesive.

Sitri looked down at Evie then up at Stolas. A flare of protectiveness skittered up my spine at the smile he gave my favored brother as he put the Stolas-and-Evie puzzle together.

A tray of champagne appeared at the table, and I grabbed two glasses at a time and handed them out. With each deposited glass, I allowed my skin to make contact with each human. A small bit of encouragement toward inebriation.

Stolas shot me a warning glance, knowing what madness I was trying to enact.

"Tiffany. Jordan. Stop, we said only three drinks," the one sitting nearest Evie shouted, but it was too late.

Each downed a second glass, then a third.

Whatever their agreement, it was as thin as a starved man's patience at a feast against the power of the Prince of Gluttony. I grinned into my glass at the crack in their friendship.

"Rhomi, lighten up. It's just a little bubbly," the blonde said before laying her head on the Watcher's chest. Her hand trailed up his neck, and she lost herself in his eyes.

Rhomi huffed and crossed her arms like a brat. "Well, you didn't have to leave your dance partner downstairs."

I admired that sort of demanding nature. I saw it in myself often, and it reminded me of the woman I'd been waiting for all night. The expectation sank into my stomach and tampered with my mood.

"I'll dance with you, darling." I offered Rhomi my hand and attention.

Rhomi stood and pulled her friends along with her, but once we got to the dance floor, her ass was pressed to my groin and all consideration of her friends was dismissed.

I allowed my thoughts to wander as the music guided my body. Amber's ass in her tight dress. The way her lip twitched during our conversation. The hitch in her breath in the last moments we'd shared.

Had I been too sure she was going to show up tonight?

I knew she'd gone home with her date, and by the quiet gestures they shared, I knew he was her sub. She had him so tuned in to her emotions that he'd felt when she needed an out. I hadn't threatened her—she would have made that very clear—but I'd gotten under her skin, and that was where I wanted to be buried until the end of time.

To live under her soft brown skin and have access to every sensitive nook of her made my cock spring to life through the haze of alcohol. I throbbed and tensed at the visions of what her hands could deliver in whatever punishment she saw fit if she knew I was thinking of her while touching some other body. The hips I gripped were frail to what I imagined Amber's would be. My hands roved over a stomach that was tight and strong, but may as well have been made of granite in comparison to the soft curve of Amber's stomach in her tight dress.

Rhomi turned in my arms and brought her mouth to mine. Her tongue tasted like ash, and her lips were too thin. Amber's were a mouthwatering hint about the pillowy lips between her thighs. Oh, how I longed to slip my fingers into Amber's wet heat and beckon her into climax with slow ministrations.

A harsh sting to my cheek roused me from my fantasy and the angry face of Rhomi tilted in my vision. Too much to drink had finally caught up to me and she stomped away. I followed her back to the booth, knowing Stolas was about to be furious with me.

She hauled her friends out of the arms of their prospective playmates and Stolas shot me a hateful glare as I sank into the booth across from him.

"Prudish bitch," I slurred, my words being drowned in

my intoxication. "She would have been lucky to have had me for a night."

"In your state, you wouldn't have stayed conscious long enough for your clothes to come off," Stolas shot back with only mild irritation, a kindness if I were being honest. "You owe me for that interruption."

"You should be thanking me." I waved a hand in the air vaguely. "I'd bet good money that she will be pounding on your door within the day to finish what had been started."

"Ten thousand," he countered, his anger surfacing.

"Twenty. If she finds you in the next"—I glanced down at his watch then back up to him with a half-hearted grin—"twelve hours, you owe me twenty thousand dollars and that pretty new sports car you won off Sitri in Vegas."

"You don't even drive."

"No. But you do."

He laughed. Not a full one, but enough that I knew he wouldn't stay mad at me for long. "You really are the worst of us."

"Tell Seere that fact when you see him, won't you? He likes to believe he is the baddest of the bad."

Stolas shook his head. There were many years when Stolas and I hadn't been able to stand each other. When being in the same room had felt like a war all its own. That was before we realized how similar we were and how we could benefit from the turn of the latest century if we teamed up. Since then, we'd been inseparable. To the point that we were neighbors in our human dwellings and rarely went a day without seeing each other.

At the office, there were rumors that our relationship transcended brotherly love, and to their human minds, it would.

We were born of light then baptized in sin. No other being on this plane could feel me as deeply as Stolas. He was the only one who saw me when I was at my darkest, most lost point. When I was swallowed whole by hopelessness and driven to my bed for months in the pursuit of rotting, Stolas dragged me kicking and screaming from my own destruction. I owed him more than my life. I owed a life full of the purpose and strength that he'd lent me until I found my own again.

I could not put that sort of love into words a human mind could comprehend, so I didn't; I would never have to because he knew.

What he also knew was that the woman who just appeared next to our booth was the reason my head lifted and my mind sobered.

"Oro." Amber greeted me with a dip of her head then turned to introduce the human she'd brought with her. "This is my friend, Veronica."

The woman at her side complemented her beautifully. Both were dark-haired, but her companion was shorter and smaller. She wore an olive-green dress to the deep purple that Amber wore. She'd brought this woman as a buffer or an escape plan, but she wouldn't need one.

As quickly as her eyes met mine, I felt my blood burning to the surface of my skin. I needed her.

I got to my feet and offered my hand to Veronica out of respect, but I would be lying if I said it was a genuine greeting. The quicker I could defer her friend to another's attention, the sooner I could get Amber to myself.

"It's a pleasure to meet you." I glanced back at Stolas, who gave me a nod of acceptance. "This is my brother, Stiles."

Offering the human name he used indicated to him that Veronica wasn't the prize in my eyes. She was free game.

He gave her a smile then signaled to a waitress. "You ladies look thirsty."

"Parched," Veronica answered, her eyes glued to my most illustrious brother.

"Maybe water, then?"

"You're funny." Amber let out a giggle and wrinkled her nose at him.

"And you are very beautiful."

He was a dead man.

Stolas grinned up at me as a tray with a bottle of champagne and accompanying glasses was dropped off.

Cheeky bastard.

Veronica sat on Stolas' left, and Amber followed. I gave my balls a metaphorical tug and took a seat on Amber's other side in the hope that she would be doing it for me later.

While Amber took a long sip from her glass, her eyes wandered over the drunken, chaotic movement on the dance floor. She was stunning. Being close enough to observe the way she existed in a room but somehow felt perfectly in control of her surroundings was mesmerizing.

"Do you dance?" I swirled the bubbles in my glass but didn't bring it to my lips. I was forcing myself to sober up so as to not make a rancid ass out of myself.

"No. But I like to watch." Her eyes flitted to mine in an intentional silent tell. "Do you dance?" she asked, allowing our conversation to expand to more than me begging for an opening.

"I would for you."

The edge of her mouth tipped, and my heart leaped.

Veronica and Stolas lulled themselves into a conversation. Stolas' attention was focused on Evie, so distracting Veronica without the prospect of taking her to bed was easy for him.

Amber's hand never left the top of Veronica's knee, anchoring her wingwoman to her side like a life raft. As our conversation moved to more casual topics, I watched which ones caused Amber's fingers to tighten and which kept her relaxed. When Stolas joined in, Amber's hand was steady. Not one question was too personal or uncomfortable. But once I started in again, every other inquiry created a small tension in her fingers. I wasn't sure what sort of poker game we were playing, but I had no intention of losing to the Prince of Greed again.

I caught Stolas' attention when Amber checked in with her friend. My brows rose, and I pointed my chin at the bar. He rolled his eyes but cleared his throat to get Veronica to face him again. "Who would like a house specialty?"

"What's the house specialty?" Veronica gazed up in pure sensuality.

"You'll see. I hope you like pineapple." He took her by the hand and led her away, leaving Amber without her blockade and giving me a chance to go in for the kill.

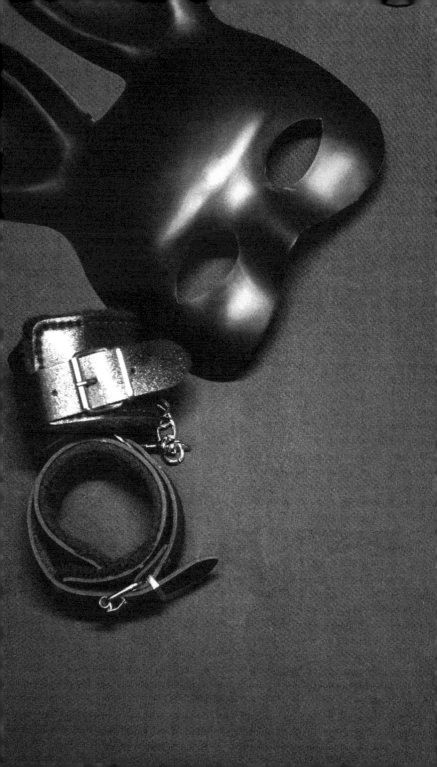

CHAPTER 6
AMBER

I shouldn't have come.

My better judgment had taken a back seat to my curiosity. It was indulgence and nothing more when I'd talked myself out of calling Sitri to ask him about Oro. I didn't want the answer to chase away the fog I was walking through. It was the way he'd pinned me for my dominant nature so quickly and immediately shifted into submissive behavior that drew me to his flame.

"You are gorgeous tonight," Oro said, the sultry tone resonating just below the music.

He was drunk, but getting to know him would be easier than when he was at his most cunning. I had the advantage with a buffer of alcohol to keep his true nature more subdued.

"I'm gorgeous every night," I countered, biting back the smile I got from his amusement.

"I never doubted it." He shifted closer but didn't press any part of himself against me. "And anyone lucky enough to see you every night has a target on his head by whoever is next in line."

"It's a long line."

"Sounds like a bloody road to trek."

The dip in his voice woke a destructive beast down in my core. My list of subs wasn't as long as he thought, but I never minded a competitive combatant. Brutality and bondage could have been coined as my specialties. Seeing a sub tied to a fuck bench and hearing the crack of a whip over flesh and muscle was enough to make my toes curl.

"Can I ask you something?" I asked.

His ears perked, and he sat straighter.

"Why do you have such interest in getting me into bed?" It was a blunt but honest question. "And don't mention how beautiful or visually appealing you find me. Flattery won't be enough of an answer."

His cat-like grin should have been a sign to run. I'd been caught in a trap I hadn't seen him lay.

"You don't treat me like the monster I am. In fact, the rush of your blood under your skin says you welcome the challenge. You're hungry for as much pleasure as a being can give you. And by the way you've tried your best to ignore me, you couldn't help giving one last look at temptation."

His final words were heavy on his tongue and teeth.

My fingers trailed up his thigh, and his breath got thicker as he continued, "You could inflict the most beautiful pain with words or your hands, but I would beg for tenfold. Because you want to see how much of my skin you can mark as your own, and make no mistake—I would turn myself inside out just to have your name on every inch of this vessel."

A flutter in my chest was threatening to turn into a proposition. Talking myself down from giving in to him was becoming harder the longer I allowed him in my company.

"I can be very pliant if that's what's worrying you," he said, his fingers finally grazing the back of my arm and stoking the fire his words had sparked.

"You could be anything you needed to be to get what you wanted."

"I could be anything you wanted for as long as you wanted."

I narrowed my eyes at him. "What do I want?"

He ran his tongue along his teeth and dropped his gaze to where his hand caressed my goose bump-covered skin.

"I won't pretend to know what you have in mind for me at this moment, but I hope leather and straps are involved."

My mind wandered to the room that Sitri always set aside for me and the tools housed there. I had plenty of straps, ropes, and impact instruments. But what he really needed was a ball gag, which I'd left in my other purse.

No.

I wasn't going to allow him to get off so easily —literally.

"Take me to your place," I said. "We'll see how well you can take direction."

He didn't question the invitation. He got to his tipsy feet and offered me his hand like the semblance of a gentleman he tried to emulate. I waved over to Veronica, a quick rehearsed gesture that meant we would be going our own ways for the rest of the night. Veronica was another domme, but new to this side of the scene. She was still too sweet on her subs, but she was a quick learner.

Oro's fingers laced into mine, and in a breath, he was pulling us through the void to the entrance of the lion's den.

CHAPTER 7
OROBAS

S he'd agreed to come with me.

No. Better yet, she had told me to bring her back to my home.

Tonight, Amber would get what she demanded. I could be obedient. I could be anything for her. If she wished, I would drain every ounce of blood and marrow from my body and replace it with her favorite perfume. At least I would be useful in her eyes.

She looked around my beachside home.

For my namesake, I didn't own much outside of fashionable necessities. I'd bought the house to be close to Stolas, but I'd become accustomed to listening to the waves outside my window at night. Nothing made me feel more at home than the sea breeze blowing through the gauzy curtains. It was a sound investment and only dimes from my pocket. The mortgage was high but not as high as the monthly bill I sent to the neighbor to keep their mouth shut about the occasional screams that came from my visitors.

Amber took her first step. Perhaps she was waiting for the dangers that went bump under the bed at night, or maybe she was admiring the priceless art I'd won off Sitri. Either way, I watched her every move, how her muscles stretched and pulled at the fabric of her dress, how her hips swayed with her every step around my living room.

Step.

Swish.

Step.

Sway.

If the room had fallen away around her, I wouldn't have noticed. The only sight worth witnessing was the garment hugging her curves and her thighs pressing together with every perfect footfall.

Her fingers trailed up her side then silently over the keys of the piano tucked in the corner of the room. Fingers I would let slit my arteries then suck clean if she worried about the mess.

"Do you play?" Her voice cut through the charged air like a bell, reminding me that I was about to be put to the test.

"Yes. Not well."

That wasn't a lie, but not fully the truth. I'd bought the piano from Arthur Rubinstein when he'd become too arthritic to play. His family had been furious until they saw their inheritance checks after he died. Before I'd taken it off his hands, he'd taught me a few things. I would never be as great as he was, but I could hold a tune in a bucket.

"Play for me," she commanded.

I watched the satisfaction play on her lips as she watched me cross the room without the smallest delay. My fingers danced over the keys while she stood watching. I played for several minutes before she bent down to my ear. "Don't stop playing until I say so."

"Yes, ma'am."

"Yes, *Miss Amber*," she corrected.

My cock was at full attention at the sternness in her voice. "Yes, Miss Amber," I repeated. I hoped I wasn't drooling like the puppy I was turning into.

She stepped up onto the bench next to me then sat on the top of the piano, sliding into my field of view, then brought a leg over my head. The glory between her thighs was partly hidden beneath the folds of her dress.

"If the music stops, then so do we. Understand?" She bent forward, planting a light kiss on my lips.

I nodded and watched her sit back. The hem of her dress skimmed up to her stomach. She was bare underneath. Her perfect pussy was on display for me. The sweet scent of her had my blood rushing from my extremities to my hard cock so fast, it swelled painfully. I leaned in, but she sat up and pulled her dress back down.

"Oro," she warned.

My fingers had stopped. I hadn't managed to reach for her yet, but I'd forgotten everything but that her perfect cunt existed moments ago.

"It won't happen again, Miss Amber." I started playing again, something slow and heart-wrenching for her.

She rewarded me by moving back into position. Her

hand smoothed down her stomach, then two fingers circled her clit to the rhythm. I carefully increased the pace of my fingers to quicken hers. The crescendo of her heavy breaths turned to small whines of pleasure and finally to an ovation that had me tipping to my own peak without release.

Her head lolled back, and I refused my body's every demand to take her on top of the instrument. Instead, I played a happier melody to give her a moment to catch her breath.

"You did so good, Oros. Ready for round two of our game?"

I nodded, careful not to drop the tempo.

She smiled and sat right on the edge of the piano and lay back until she was splayed wide before me. The heels of her shoes rested on the keys on either side of me. My hands, still playing between her feet, ached to make their way up her calves toward her wet center.

"You can taste but the music can't stop," she commanded.

"Do you have any requests?" I tapped my fingers quickly for an upbeat tune.

"Something slow."

I smiled to myself and transitioned to a melody. Amber kept her arms up by her head, which gave me free rein to start wherever my tongue pleased. I kissed the inside of one knee, then the other. She hummed in approval, and I inched higher with every encouraging moan.

I got to the apex of her thighs and took a moment to savor the rise and fall of her chest. The gift I so freely unleashed upon this plane pumped through my body like the ebb of the ocean currents on rocky shores. The beating of power under my skin mimed the pounding of her heart, a connection I couldn't have made even if I tried. Sometimes, I wondered if it had a life of its own and I was merely the product of the puppeteer.

Reeling in that hunger, I flattened my tongue against the tender nook of her leg. She let out a sigh. I waited for her to inhale before I plunged my tongue into her cunt. My fingers played across the keys, the melody staying stable while her pleasure mounted from the swirling and sucking of my mouth. The nectar of the goddesses awakened my taste buds and brought a moan of gratitude to my unworthy lips.

It was poetic. Amber was being devoured by a beast to the mellifluous tones of "Vladimir's Blues." I chose this song because there were sections I could play with one free hand, and as her thighs clenched around my neck, I slipped two fingers inside her. While one hand played another chorus, the other brought her to the edge of her climax with firm, hard thrusts.

"Oh fuck," she sang out slowly, and her walls squeezed around me.

She came down from her high, and I returned to regaling her with all ten fingers on the keys. Her release coated the ivory.

When her senses returned, she sat up and looked down at me with spent lust in her gaze. I stopped playing and waited for her next instructions, savoring the heat between us.

Satiation by me looked glorious on her.

Wordlessly, she dropped into my lap. The heat between her legs landed on my cock, where it belonged. I kept my hands to my sides, waiting for her permission to touch her. Our scene may have been over, but if I lost control now, she would never see me again.

She wrapped her arms around my neck and leaned in close to lick the taste of her own pleasure from my lips.

"I have an early morning," she said between light kisses.

"When can I see you again?" I sounded just as desperate as the gnawing animal in my chest felt.

"Hmm." She rolled her head back, the swells of her breasts tempting my teeth. "Tomorrow night. My place."

"I'll be there."

I was left alone with a throbbing cock but only the taste for more of her on my mind. I took her back to the front of The Deacon, where her car service was waiting. We exchanged phone numbers and then she was gone into the night. I could have gone into the club and procured a decent enough replacement, but no other body would satiate me the way the thought of her and my own hand would.

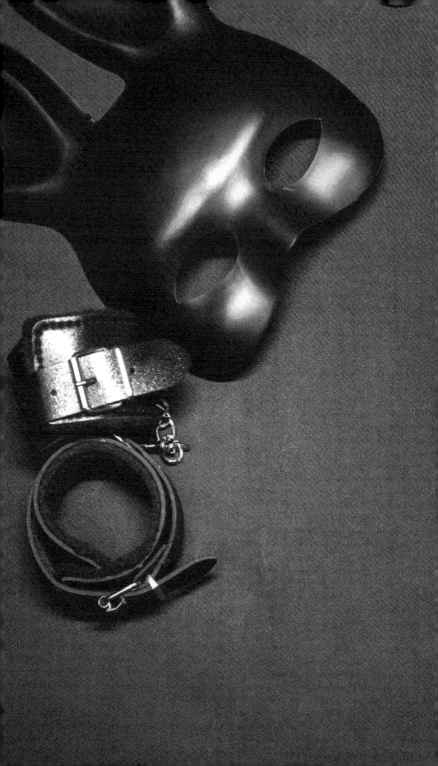

CHAPTER 8
AMBER

On my way home, I checked my notifications. Two of my subs had sent me messages and cash deposits.

SIMONS

I miss you.

AMBER

You always miss me.

A notification for a five-hundred-dollar deposit dropped at the top of my screen. Then another text message.

SIMONS

I bought another boat today. Thinking of naming it after you. The Amber Dawn.

AMBER

You're such a wasteful asshole.

SIMONS

I put it in your name. I'm thinking of taking you to Paris next weekend. The finest hotels and restaurants. Then shopping at your favorite designers.

AMBER

Another irresponsible and frivolous trip.

SIMONS

However much you spend, I'll deposit in your account.

AMBER

Pathetic puppet.

SIMONS

Yes, ma'am.

Another deposit alert. This time for one thousand dollars.

AMBER

See you next week. My favorite champagne only on the flight. And if you want to play, it better be a private jet.

SIMONS

I'll go plane shopping in the morning.

I rolled my eyes and moved on to my next sub's messages:

ALLEN

I can't serve you this week. I have a work trip to Toronto.

That explained the three-hundred-dollar deposit from him. He and I didn't normally have a financial relationship like Simons and I did. Allen was more modest and worked a white-collar job as a mundane accountant.

Simons owned too many companies around the world and did none of the work, which was why he got off on spending his wealth on me and listening to me berate him about it. Simons slept around with whoever would oblige but was only financially tied to me. Our relationship was physical, but he salivated at the idea of having me on his arm in public.

I was his crown jewel at every party Simons attended. It was where I'd met many others in our lifestyle, and those connections had brought me to The Deacon. Sitri was the center of a lot of connections, I realized. Or perhaps demons in general had many overlapping acquaintances.

I wondered how Oro fit into that dynamic as I pulled up to my house. The driver hopped out, opened the door for me, then followed me up the walkway. He was a gentleman if there ever was one and a bodyguard when I needed him.

"Thank you, Hank. I'll call you tomorrow if there is any change to my schedule."

He nodded but waited for me to unlock the door and for the lights inside to flick on before heading back to the car to wait until I sent a good-night text.

Having signals with everyone in my circle was for my and their safety. Hank had been hired after the second stalker had broken into my house after disarming the alarm system.

Thank fuck for Hank. He'd saved my life several times since coming into my service and was paid very well to do so.

I had a few errands to run the next day but had a free evening, which was now occupied by a demon who had made me come so hard, I saw stars. But he hadn't used his abilities to do so. It had been all raw skill, tongue, and fingers. And for that, it was my turn to treat him to an orgasm he'd never forget.

CHAPTER 9
OROBAS

S tolas paced his living room. He had a date the next day with Evie and the nerves were getting to him.

"What is the matter with you? You're acting like you've never fucked a human before." I stretched my arms over my head, driving my own anticipation away for the moment.

"What if she doesn't show up?"

"Then you storm the castle, take the girl, and slay the dragon in your most shiny suit. The Prada one, if my choice is being considered."

He side-eyed me.

"She can't run from you, Stolas. Her soul is branded with your name," I reminded him.

"I want her to agree to help me willingly. It has to be her choice," he said for the fourth time.

I flicked the lint from my trousers. "If you'd slept with her last night, your mutual daddy issues could have been aired out already."

"What daddy issues?" Sitri chimed in, appearing from the void. "I don't have daddy issues."

"Speak for yourself, oh-gluttonous-one," Stolas remarked.

"Of course you have daddy issues. We all do. What else would you call being kicked out of our home then spending the rest of time trying to prove our Father wrong or right?" I held up both hands in exasperation. "What are you doing here, Sitri?"

Stolas shot our brother a furrowed glance as well. "What *are* you doing here?"

Sitri blew out a sigh and his shoulders dropped. "The Reaper—"

"You owe me that bungalow in Brooklyn." Stolas pointed at me sharply.

"Fucking hell, Sitri," I grumbled. "You couldn't wait one more day to fuck her?" I pulled out my key ring then tossed Stolas the key to one of my favorite hideaways.

"You're both assholes." Sitri dragged a hand down his face.

"All right, sorry." I squared my leg up on the couch to turn my full attention to him. "Brotherly love time. What's the problem?"

"Such an asshole," Sitri said under his breath. "Having her around feels . . . right. I think Ezequiel is getting too attached, but she isn't meant for his plane."

Stolas and I shared a look. A silent remark of skepticism that Ezequiel was the only one getting attached.

"It sounds like the problem will resolve itself," I stated. "Once her work here is done, she will go where she belongs, and you will be free of her and his attention will be back on only you."

"I'm not jealous of them!" Sitri practically shouted.

Stolas gave him a facial expression that said, "Sure, keep telling yourself that."

"Ignore her," I offered.

Sitri scoffed. "Coming from you, that's rich."

"Thank you." I smiled up at him, cocksure.

"I came to talk to Stolas," Sitri admitted and turned his broad shoulder to me. "After the display he put on last night with your mutual friend, I assumed he'd have sage advice for me."

"You break my heart, brother," I said. "I am as sage and wise as Stolas. And twice as good-looking."

"You once dressed a pig in a nightgown," Stolas recollected, "and let it loose in the Welsh king's chambers because you fancied his second wife and thought he wouldn't notice she was gone for the night."

I held up a finger in my defense. "He only noticed after sticking his cock in and it squealed for him like she only ever did for me."

"Vile creature." Sitri wrinkled his nose.

"The king or the pig?" I asked. "Pigs are quite sweet if you get to know them."

"I meant you." Sitri flung a pillow at me, hitting the side of my face and causing a snicker of laughter from Stolas.

I hurled it back at Sitri, and he hugged it to his deflated chest.

Stolas composed himself then turned into our level-headed prince. "Did you fuck her for fun or out of frustration?"

"A little of both." Sitri rolled his eyes up to the ceiling.

"Was it good?" I asked, but Sitri didn't answer.

"Is she out of your system?" Stolas continued.

Sitri sat with this question for a moment, which was more of a true answer than the one he gave finally. "Yes."

Stolas and I both knew there was no such thing when it came to us. Lust, greed, and gluttony were bottomless pits of indulgence. Harmless if you thought about it. How could too much sex, money, or desire hurt?

"She will be gone soon and so will the temptation. Just hold out until then." Stolas' hushed voice reached across the room, but so did his ability to soothe and comfort.

"Death's ferrymen are not meant to be embodied and partake in our novelties." My remark echoed my earlier statement, but I hoped it dug itself deeper into Sitri's brain this time around.

"Right," Sitri said after a long pause. "I have to get back to the club. Thank you, Stolas."

"Anytime, brother." Stolas crossed the room and embraced Sitri. I could have sworn I heard him whisper something but didn't catch it.

Sitri pulled away with a nod and disappeared into the void. If he got what he came for, I didn't know for sure, but his visit calmed Stolas enough that we could go to the gym together and work out our own current plagues with grunts and weights.

CHAPTER 10
AMBER

O ro texted that he would be here at 8 o'clock.
I had plenty of time to set our scene for the night. He'd been on his best behavior last time, so I thought I'd give him a more challenging request. I tightened the ropes, pulls, and leather straps to the bed, then pulled the pillows off. He would need all the range of motion he could get without impediments.

When I was done in my bedroom, I went to the kitchen and poured two glasses of whiskey. I scrolled through our minimal text threat. Just a quick hello and my address for the evening's events—and the message that made my heart melt.

ORO

> Thousands of years of endless living and I've never been more excited to see someone. Until tonight. Xoxo

I let the butterflies squirm in my belly. It was so rare

that prep for a scene made me giddy. There was a state of comfort in being in complete control. My current partners had their special requests and preferences when we were together, but how and when they reached ecstasy was always my choosing. I knew it would be different with Oro but had no clue how.

The doorbell rang, surprising me. He could have appeared in my living room if he had wanted.

The door swung open, and the embodiment of sin filled the frame. I'd half expected to find him standing awkwardly on my front step, but of course not. His dark hair was slicked back, several of the buttons on his white shirt were undone, and his tan linen slacks were tailored to fit him effortlessly.

My mouth watered. I couldn't wait to turn his clean, crisp appearance into a rutty mess.

"I hope I'm not late." He broke my gawking stare and took a step over the threshold.

"Early actually."

I moved aside to invite him in. Like the gentleman he seemed to be possessing, he waited for me to lead us deeper into my house. In the living room, I waved to the couch to offer him a seat. He sat like a good boy and was rewarded with a drink in his hand.

His eyes taking note of every corner of my body didn't go unnoticed, and I wondered what he was thinking. Was he prepared for what I had planned for us this evening?

We were about to find out.

He watched me over the rim of his glass, finishing the amber liquor in one greedy gulp then setting it on the center table. I took a long pull from my own, drawing out his anticipation and edging his curiosity. It would be the theme of the evening, so he was getting a small taste.

I swallowed down my nervous energy—and alcohol—then cleared my throat.

"What do you have on the menu for me tonight?" His eyes stayed on mine in a battle of wills, not with me but with his own cravings.

"You said you were flexible, right?" I got to my feet, and he got to his immediately. "I thought we would test your limits. Physically at first. Then we'll see how far you'll allow me to push you until you can't take any more."

He smirked. "I'm all aflutter."

The scene was set, but there was one last part we had to go over before I opened the door to my bedroom. "I like to go by the light system. Green for 'yes, Miss Amber, give me more,' yellow for breaks and readjustments, and red for stop the scene."

"Understood." He ran a finger down my cheek and tilted my chin up. His lips brushed over mine. "I trust you, Miss Amber."

My center pulsed at the use of his name for me. His consent and eagerness sent electricity over my skin as I broke away from his heated gaze and opened the door. I watched his expression change from docile to viciously pleased.

"Where do you want me?" He looked back at me with a expression that threatened to set me ablaze.

"First, your clothes and shoes can go there." I pointed

to a chair in the corner. "Then, make yourself comfortable in the middle of the mattress."

He nodded, crossing the room and turning his back to me as he slowly took each article of clothing off, folded it neatly, and set it on the chair. His ass was as smooth as marble, and my crop would chisel it into masterful art. When he finally turned around, my jaw went slack. His body was a reminder that he was once sculpted by God then driven to Earth to commit and inspire devastating sins.

I untied my dress and let it fall to the floor, revealing my own battle gear: a shiny leather corset and straps around my waist that would hold whatever toy I chose for later. My eyes moved from his to the bed, a silent instruction that he took without a second thought. He settled with his arms above his head and feet apart, waiting for his restraints.

There were many times when I'd enjoyed strapping men to my bed and twisting their pleasures until they were in tears for relief, but none was as exciting as the soft caress of Oro's fingers over my palms as I cinched the clasps around his wrists.

He realized there was a pulley system in place down by his ankles, and that made his breath hitch at the first crank. His feet lifted off the bed several inches. After he settled his back into the new position, I pulled again until his heels were directly over his head.

"How's the stretch?" I smoothed my hand over his ass and up between his thighs to his calves.

His cock hardened at my voice. "As green as could be, Miss Amber."

"Good."

The ropes tightened again, and his legs folded over his torso. He let out a groan and adjusted himself again. I stroked his shaft and he thickened at my touch. A bead of excitement formed on the tip of his cock for me. My thumb massaged the viscous liquid over his swollen head. He struggled to take a deep enough breath but managed to whimper when I added more pressure.

"Stick out your tongue," I ordered, and he obeyed.

I took a mental measurement then lifted his lower half higher until his cock easily sat at his mouth. He wasn't joking about being flexible. Any other man would have cried for mercy by now, but Oro was watching me with a silent plea for more. He wanted me to push his limits until *I* was coming apart.

One last pull of the ropes and we were ready.

"You're going to suck your own dick while I use you, but no coming until I say so, agreed?"

He nodded, his cock bobbing on his tongue before his lips circled around his shaft. My pussy throbbed at the sight. I gave his upturned ass a solid smack from my palm and he moaned.

I opened my side table to retrieve a bottle of lube, a dildo for my strap, and my tightest riding crop. His eyes bulged at the phallus I was attaching to my groin. It was no bigger than he was but still impressive. I squeezed lube onto the glass shaft then put a little extra in my hand. His greedy hole would be prepped before I had my way with him.

When I stood on the bed above him, I took a moment to enjoy the puzzle I'd made of him. He was contorted and strung up so beautifully for me.

I held the riding crop under my arm to free my hands so I could circle his tight hole and cup his balls with the other. I gave him a gentle squeeze as I pushed my finger inside. Once he'd become accustomed to the stretch, I let go of his sack and gripped my crop. I brought it over my head then down over the taut skin at the back of his thigh. The welt rose hot and red within seconds.

"Mmm," he groaned around his shaft.

"More?" I lifted the crop again, ready to strike.

He pulled away to speak, his voice desperate already. "Please, more. Please, Miss Amber. Fuck."

With a sharp crack on his ass, he let out a yelp. He huffed and took the pain until it melted into pleasure. I shoved a second finger into his ass and stroked his shaft. His head fell back and he hissed his satisfaction. My heart-beat quickened. Edging him closer to madness and being the commander of his pleasure tightened my core.

His cock pulsed in my hand. He was getting too close to coming already, so I took a handful of his hair and forced his head up.

"Suck this big cock for me."

His mouth opened wide, engulfing his red, engorged tip. He hollowed his cheeks as he drew himself deeper. The ring of muscle around my two fingers pulsed. Pushing my digits apart, I added a third. The fullness brought another whimper from his full mouth.

"Time for something bigger," I said.

He mumbled a word that resembled "green" and nodded eagerly. Though I knew he could handle being pegged, I added another dollop of lubricant to the dildo attached to my leather garment. The underwear I wore housed a vibrating pad—a little something for the wearer to enjoy while their playmate got off. I turned it on then sank the gleaming glass dick into him.

His eyes rolled to the back of his head and his jaw slacked. His cock bobbed out of his mouth, and he dripped saliva onto his lips.

"Fuck me," he groaned. His hips attempted to grind against me, but he had nowhere to go in his restraints.

"Not yet." I sank down deeper. "You have to beg for it."

I forced the tip of his cock back into his mouth. His lips were red from the work he'd been putting in. The sweat on his forehead dampened his hair, making the waves come loose from the styling gel. The pattern of where my crop had been made him look used and wanton.

He was perfect.

He whimpered and whined as I fucked his tight hole slowly. The vibration from my strap-on and the way his brows drew together brought me closer to orgasm with every movement. I bore down until the hilt of my toy was flush against his ass. I moaned. My clit throbbed and my walls convulsed.

His hungry eyes watched me come, a mix of emotions painted on his pleasure-tortured face. I pulled out of him then plunged into him again. My hips slapped against his ass cheeks, forcing his cock down his throat with every thrust. His eyes glazed over as my rhythm brought him closer to the edge.

"Do you want to come, darling?" My husky voice broke through his muffled sounds of ecstasy.

"Mhmm."

I took a firm hold of the base of his cock, pumping for him. "Beg for it."

"Please. Let me come. Please. Oh fuck, Miss Amber. I need to come." He whimpered and my pussy pulsed, another orgasm mounting. "Harder. Fuck me harder. Please."

I withdrew the dildo to the tip and slammed inside of him. My fist on his cock moved faster. His clipped breathing quickened, and his brow furrowed with his concentration.

"Open your mouth," I demanded, shoving his throbbing tip between his lips. "I want you to taste yourself."

He opened wide, his tongue becoming a flat platform for his release. My hips faltered at his obedience. The sight of his cum gushing from the tip of his cock pushed me over the edge of my orgasm. He lapped at the thick white substance, not wasting one drop.

"You did so good, Oro." I smoothed a lock of hair from his eye.

His head lolled back from exhaustion. While he came down from his high, I pulled out of him and quickly loosened the ropes. His body sprawled out on the mussed sheets, his chest heaving to bring fresh air to his spent muscles. The skin was red around where the ropes and leather had been.

Our scene was over, but this was my favorite part. I opened the linen warmer next to my bed that held a robe and a small blanket for aftercare purposes. He wasn't shivering yet but likely would from the expended energy.

I went to the bathroom to wash my hands and left the toy in the sink to be washed. Then, I went back into the bedroom with a wet washrag. To my surprise, he was sitting on the edge of the bed in the robe.

"That was incredible." He sighed, euphoria glowing on his face.

I handed him the washcloth, and he wiped tears, saliva, and cum from his face.

"Have you ever had too much?" I asked. "It seems like you don't have a limit when it comes to sex."

He wasn't offended, but there was a moment when I thought I saw disappointment. "Glad I could be a pleasant wonderment for you."

He wrapped his arms around my hips, clasping his hands on my ass to bring my stomach toward his face. The warmth of his skin heated mine, and I debated getting naked just to feel his touch.

I raked my fingers through his hair, the dark waves rebelling back to his brow. "It was a compliment," I tried to clarify.

His chin pressed into the smooth leather of my corset and our eyes locked. "My existence is excess. Every cell of this body was made to be pushed to the brink and beyond. I can never get enough."

"That sounds exhausting." My brows stitched together, the pity plain on my face. "And frustrating."

His hands trailed down my thighs to the backs of my knees then pulled until I straddled his lap. He leaned over and kissed the swells of my breasts before looking back up at me through heavy, spent lids.

"You can imagine my chagrin when you gave me what I have been hunting for so many lifetimes. Through centuries of orgies and the creation of kinks so blasphemous that the Church deemed them worthy of Hell. Yet meeting you has fed my soul in ways I thought were only myth."

My heart sank in my chest.

I tangled my fingers in his hair and cupped the back of his head. My lips parted to tease his tongue. His arms around my waist tightened, bringing my core down onto him. I expected to find him hard again, but he wasn't. That was possibly the most telling part of our whole evening.

"Thank you." He pressed his lips to mine in a soft, hesitant kiss.

CHAPTER 11
OROBAS

She let me kiss and hold her through the night. I knew I fell asleep first because the lights in the house were off when I woke up hours later. Her soft breathing next to me was a gift I didn't earn, but I would enjoy it for as long as I could. She was so beautiful when she slept, but it was the memory of her mounted on top of me that stirred my urge to touch her.

Slipping my hand under the hem of her gown, I brushed the pads of my fingers over the soft skin between her thighs. She rolled into my touch, her back flush to the mattress and her knees parting so graciously for me.

I ran my thumb up her warm slit, massaging her clit until wetness seeped from her core. I rubbed the slickness over her pussy slowly, not wanting to wake her fully. Her nipples pebbled under her clothing, giving my tongue a target. Doming over her small breast, I flicked my tongue over the hard nub and soaked the spot.

She sighed in her sleep, and her thighs clenched

around my hand. Her hips searched for the source of the friction, and my fingers answered with more pressure. The pulsing of her pussy begged for me to focus on her needy entrance, so I used two fingers to press against the tight opening but didn't dare to go deeper until she let out a frustrated groan. Both fingers slipped inside. If she wanted more of me, she would demand it.

The current of her hips worked her pussy around my digits until she was biting her lip and whimpering for release. A need in my belly clenched, like I was suddenly jealous of my own hand.

I needed to taste her. My fingers retreated, and her thighs relaxed enough for me to move under the blanket and settle between her legs. Her foot smoothed up my back, her subconscious giving me permission to give her more.

We had discussed this particular scenario during our conversations about hard and soft limits. Mostly hers. I drew the line at animal suits or livestock, which she'd agreed to with a giggle that made my toes curl. I wanted to please this woman on every level. And being woken by a lover was on her list of grey. After the evening we shared, I'd surely earned a chance to surprise her.

Looping my arms under her hips, I used two fingers to frame her clit for me. I stuck my tongue out and lashed it back and forth over her swelling bundle. Between soft suckles and quick flicks, I circled her entrance with two fingertips, careful not to enter without her consent.

"Oh God." Her husky, sleep-drunk voice cracked somewhere in the dark.

I took her clit between my teeth and rolled it until her legs jerked. "Don't speak His name. Only mine."

"Oro," she moaned, her hand seeking me under the blanket and sinking into my hair.

She held me firm and ground her cunt over my mouth. Her delicious essence coated my lips, chin, and cheeks. I moved my hands under her ass to lift her closer. I was ready to devour her but held myself back.

"Please, Miss Amber." My fingers nudged against her core. "I need to be inside of you."

"Yes," she forced out, tightening her grip on my hair.

"Can I fill you with my fingers and suck on this pretty clit until you make a mess?" I pulled back, waiting for her frustration to come to a head.

"Oro." Her firm voice was turning into a desperate whine, and suddenly all I needed in the world was for her to demand what she wanted.

"Please, let me taste. I know your pussy coming on my tongue will be so sweet."

"Fuck." Her words were strangled with lust.

"I could make you come, Miss Amber. Please let me make you come all over my face."

"Make me come, Oro." Another set of fingers weaved through my hair to pull me where she needed me.

My devious grin curled around my words. "Yes, Miss Amber."

I became ravenous, sucking, licking, and fucking her with my fingers until she gushed. Until she screamed my name and her legs shook from the force of her first orgasm. I was determined to get at least one more from her before we were through for the night.

She pulled the blankets away and guided me up her body by the back of my neck. Our mouths collided, and she sucked her juices from my tongue and lips. The sound of my need echoed into her. Her hand curled the base of my thickening cock and lined me up to her sopping-wet center. I pulsed my hips, wanting to give her a moment to change her mind, but her nails dug into my ass cheek.

"Do you want to fuck me, Oro?"

"Yes." The head of my cock throbbed against her.

"Oro. Where have your manners gone?"

I took a deep breath, reeling myself in and remembering my place. "I want to fuck this perfect pussy, Miss Amber. I want to fuck it hard and raw."

She raised her hips, letting the head of my cock slip into her tight cunt. A gruff sound vibrated in my chest. I beat down the rapidly growing hunger that threatened to take over my senses. She bucked beneath me, beckoning me. My shaft sank until I was fully seated inside of her.

Heavenly.

Pure pleasure surged through my blood.

My shoulders loosened, and I collapsed on her chest. I withdrew and thrust in again, a blinding light bursting behind my squeezed eyelids. A trance took me under the spell of this woman. A voice that sounded like my own groveled for more. Over and over, I begged. Her fingernails dug into my back, holding on while I fucked her with every ounce of energy I had left.

A symphony of my pleas and her screams of pleasure

filled my ears until my balls tightened and my gut clenched.

"Can I come, Miss Amber? Please, let me come."

"Yes, oh fuck. Come for me, Oro. Come."

My cock jerked and my release filled her pulsating pussy until it spilled out of her and pooled on the sheets. Her mouth took mine, and it set my soul alight with a flame so bright that I felt it burning under my skin, trying to escape and shine affectionately for her. I felt her soul weaving its way into the cavities of my body, felt her occupy every bone and vessel within me, driving all other purpose but providing her with pleasure from my being.

My broken and fragmented ghost would forever haunt her sheets.

She freed me from the burden of existing for any other experience that didn't include forcing my name from her gasping lips. I was hers so thoroughly that it was a miracle I had ever breathed air that she hadn't touched.

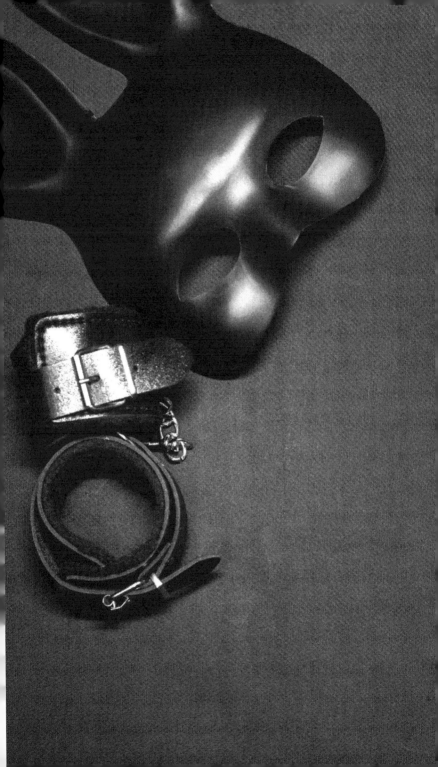

CHAPTER 12
AMBER

I was still floating on the high from my night with Orobas when I walked into The Deacon on Tuesday evening.

Sitri was pouring a mixture into a shaker while a pretty woman kissed Ezequiel on the cheek then walked away. It looked like she was heading to the elevator and up to Sitri's loft.

"Care for a drink before you whip men into submission?" Sitri's lips tipped up into a scandalous smile.

"Dirty martini. Two olives," I answered, bellying up to the bar next to Ezequiel, who was sipping on a beer.

Sitri winked. "I love it when you're demanding."

I wrinkled my nose at him, and he poured the drink into the frosted martini glass in front of me. Sitri knew how to make more drinks than any bartender I knew. I supposed he'd have learned the trends through all the decades he'd been around. Lucky for me, he made a damn fine dirty martini.

"Sitri, do you know every demon that comes to the club?" I asked.

"I do." The instant curiosity in his voice made my belly squirm.

"Has a demon stepped out of line?" Ezequiel cut in, his protective nature shining through like armor.

"No. In fact, he has been very well trained." I smiled into my drink, took a steadying sip, and went on to what I needed to ask. "His name is Oro."

"Oro?" both Sitri and Ezequiel answered.

"Yes? Should I have kept my distance?" I looked between them, and they passed unspoken words as if trying to decide what the right answer was.

"My brother can be . . . "—Sitri tiptoed over the explanation—"excessive."

"He's your brother as in—"

"A fellow prince of Hell," Ezequiel finished.

I felt sick.

"He can be potent if a human is exposed for too long. The Prince of Gluttony is a dangerous being to be around unsupervised." Ezequiel's voice was being drowned out by my panic.

Fucking Oro had been intense, more so than when I'd hooked up with Sitri. But I wouldn't have guessed that Oro contained the type of power that Sitri did.

Sitri used his influence to fill everyone around him with blind lust. It released desires that would otherwise have gone unspoken and brought the darkest kinks to the surface. He also knew hidden pleasures of the human body that I never would have guessed would be erotic.

Oro was different. There had been something lurking below the surface, but I'd assumed he had been holding back his demonic power in the pursuit of getting laid.

What had I gotten myself into? And why would a prince of sin—the Prince of Gluttony, no less—become a submissive for me on multiple occasions?

"Amber?" Ezequiel placed a hand on my shoulder and gently shook me from my thoughts.

"I'm fine," I lied. "I didn't realize who he was. He didn't disclose that to me when we talked."

That part was beginning to gnaw at me the most. We'd spent hours touching, talking, and fucking, but he never admitted his position in the hierarchy of Hell.

"You've talked?" Ezequiel laughed. "I don't know the last time I saw him talk to a human he wasn't balls deep in. Even then, he doesn't normally speak to the holes he's occupying."

They passed another skeptical silence between them, and then Sitri pinned me with a look that told me his brain had caught up to the situation.

"Did you . . ." Sitri narrowed his eyes at me.

"What?" I took a longer sip.

"You did." Ezequiel's smile curled up across his face, his bright white teeth gleaming in the overhead lights. His angelic face was full of scrutiny and mischief.

"Stop. You know that is none of your business," I scolded.

"That is where you are wrong," Sitri chimed in. "He is my brother, fellow prince, and investor in every one of my businesses. So I do have a stake in this."

"If you break it, you buy it," Ezequiel said with a wink.

"You're enjoying this too much, angel," I retorted, giving him a scowl.

He shrugged, the bright inner light of his eyes not dulling in the slightest at my withering stare.

"Is he really that bad, Sitri?" I stifled the desperation in my voice but doubted I hid it well from my face.

"Orobas holds his title for a reason, Amber," Sitri said. "During the Fall, he went days covered in the fresh blood of our brothers. He did not tire. He did not weaken. When it looked like the battle was turning against us, he held the line of attack until Lucifer finally called us to our new home. His soul is more scarred than the rest of ours, but we owe our existence in part to his refusal to surrender."

My mouth went dry.

"His gluttonous influences pale in comparison to how fierce he was in combat," Sitri continued. "When the war ended, he started a celebration that only ended when every last heart had stopped beating from exhaustion and dehydration. He doesn't just have a natural inscient for excess. He draws power from it. His soul feeds off the anguish of humans' overindulgence into their deepest desires."

Every word made my stomach churn.

Was that what he was doing with me? Indulging my every fantasy to eventually drain my life force dry only to further his own strength?

Why hadn't he done so already?

I couldn't breathe, let alone pull syllables together to form a response. I knew Sitri wouldn't lie to me, but I really wish he were. Tears stabbed behind my eyes. It was too much. I downed the rest of my drink then stood and turned away from Ezequiel and Sitri.

"Amber," Sitri called after me.

"I'm fine," I answered, but the crack in my voice echoed around the empty club as I made my way to the lockers to get my things.

"We can't help you if you don't tell us what's wrong." Ezequiel's startlingly close timbre practically made me jump out of my skin.

"He didn't do anything wrong. I did."

With that, I shut my locker then slammed the front door behind me.

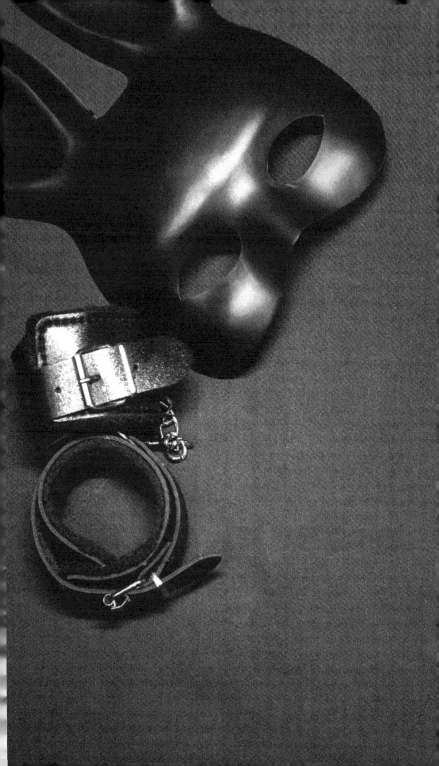

CHAPTER 13
OROBAS

My phone buzzed on my nightstand with another incoming call. Probably the fourth one since I'd reluctantly woken up. I hated being dragged from sleep.

"What?" I finally answered, putting the caller on speakerphone, refusing to sit up yet.

"I suggest you come to The Deacon before Sitri guts you in your home."

The Watcher.

I rolled my eyes. "Why isn't he the one calling me if he's threatening my bowels?"

"He's already called you six times. I'm doing you a courtesy by giving you one last chance to answer." His airy vocality made my head pound.

"I'll be there in an hour." I thumbed the call to a close without letting him utter another word.

The sun was annoyingly bright through my bedroom windows, which meant I had missed my morning fitness

97

training appointment and would likely face scrutiny from Stolas about missing work. It didn't happen often, but he was a stickler for timeliness.

I loved my job. Not the humanistic peddling of corporate funds from one large bank account to another, but sinking my teeth into our clients to urge them to the brink to watch them flail off the edge of their civility. Making men into monsters satiated a hunger I'd felt all my existence.

That was . . . until I'd tasted Miss Amber.

My cock throbbed beneath the sheets. I groaned as I stretched, doing my best to chaste the carnal need for her flesh slapping against mine. Her succulent lips around my shaft would have been the preferred way to start my day, but my hand would have to do.

I STEPPED through the void into The Deacon only thirty minutes after my call with Ezequiel. The visions of Miss Amber while I pleasured myself gratified me enough for the moment, but I was counting down until Sitri was finished berating me for whatever I'd done to anger him.

Sitri was in the office when I arrived. His enflamed eyes followed me into the room and to the sofa like I was dead meat.

"What's this about?" I gestured around, looking for some source of his ferocity.

"Did you know the club hosted a BDSM night?" Sitri started, his stern voice sounding too much like Lucifer's.

"I am aware."

I'd offered on countless occasions to turn The Deacon into a sex club, but Sitri never took me up on the idea.

"Do you know who runs the events?"

"Unfortunately for them, no. Though I bet he knows how to put on a good show."

"She," Sitri corrected.

"Okay then. She knows how to put on a good show . . . .What am I missing?"

He stood from his leather wingback chair and leaned over the desk on his knuckles. "I rarely tolerate the presence of mortals, but this one in particular I have a kinship with, and if you fuck that up, I will personally use your brain matter as a new wall decoration."

His blond waves fell over his brow, bringing forth the sinister aura that I'd only ever seen when he was willing to kill.

Though his threat was full of the heat of his rage, I couldn't stop my lips from twitching into a smile. "You're becoming so soft on them after too many years of mingling, Sitri. Who is this human woman you are so insistent that I have scorned?"

"Amber Delico."

"Amber—"

"Didn't care to get her name before destroying a powerful ally?" he seethed.

I got to my feet, no longer caring about his accusations. If she was in pain somewhere because of me, I had to find her. Beg her for forgiveness on my knees until they were bloody.

"Orobas!"

My own name followed me through the void to her front steps. I pounded my fist on the door and called out for her to answer until a pair of arms hauled me from the stoop. The air was knocked from my lungs as concrete and gravel bit into the side of my head.

"Hank." A calm voice cut through the chaos.

"Amber, please. I didn't mean to hurt you. Please," I ground out through my teeth, the knee on my back making it hard to breathe.

"You lied to me, Orobas."

A sharp pain shot through me, and it had nothing to do with the dirt being forced into my mouth or the brut digging his fists into my skull.

"You should have told me your status. You're not just some demon. You're a prince of Hell."

"Please—"

"The kind of power you hold can't be contained, and I won't risk my own life or sanity for a power dynamic that can never be balanced or someone who could lose control and kill me in an instant."

"I would never—"

"You would. That's your big gift, isn't it? Gluttony.

Excess. Bleeding a soul dry then leaving their shell for the vultures."

Frustration welled up inside of me. The pressure in my head was ready to combust, but if I did, I would be taking her bodyguard out with half the block.

I reared up, knocking the man back, and then bucked forward, sending him into the walking path face-first. He grunted in pain then yelped when I kicked him in the ribs, cracking at least three.

I turned on Amber, catching my ragged breath. "I am all those things. I have never hidden that I have the capability to ruin everything I get my teeth on, but you are different."

"How convenient." She crossed her arms and took a step into her doorway. Away from me.

"If I wanted you drooling and mindlessly sucking my cock like it was a fucking popsicle, I would have done so already."

"You will get bored of playing the submissive. Then what will stop you from fulfilling that promise?"

"Nothing about our time together was pretend."

"Stop. Just stop." For the first time, she raised her voice above the strict and practiced domme persona.

I reached out, grabbed her hip, then waited for her to recoil. But she only stiffened in my hold.

"I know what you felt, the warmth of ease and comfort in my arms. I could taste the need and hunger while I begged for my name to grace your lips." I stared down into her bronze eyes, searching for confirmation. "Please don't do this to me. Don't take away the one glimpse of contentment I've ever felt. Don't make me live without you."

"Oro—" She shook her head, tears falling down her red cheeks.

"Tell me what to do. Anything. Do you want me to kneel by your bed every day and night? Do you need me to crawl on all fours behind you to replace any chair you'd ever use? Say the word and I will chew through my wrists and never touch another living being. Please need me. Use me. Take me for your own and never let go."

She finally melted into me as her body shook against my chest.

I leaned down to meet her watery eyes. "Make me yours."

"I can't." Her sob hammered into my chest and cracked the cage surrounding my heart.

"If anyone can, it's you. I need it to be you."

The strain of her silence against my eardrums splintered the remaining cord of my restraint.

"I'm sorry."

The weight of her words dropped a thousand pounds of sorrow onto my chest, crushing any hope I had. She pulled out of my grief-stricken hands and shut the door.

"Open up." The pounding at my bedroom door got louder and louder. One fist had turned to two. "Orobas!"

The ceiling spun overhead. Whatever cocktail of pills and powders I'd taken had numbed the pain, but only while I slept. Fresh torture affronted me when the intoxication wore thin, allowing my consciousness to peak.

My body jerked before my brain caught up to the loud crashing sound then the dancing of splintered wood in the air. Stolas' face weaved in and out of focus. There was no mistaking the look of fury in his eyes.

"What the fuck happened to you?"

I blinked slowly. My tongue dragged over my dry, cracked lips and caught on the sharp, jagged skin. The grit in my eyes from days of sleep and no water felt like I was blinking with sandpaper.

"Leave me," I managed to grunt out.

"Not a chance." Stolas hoisted me by the arm out of my bed.

The sun stung my eyes, and my feet dragged over the carpet then onto the smooth, cool marble of the bathroom. He didn't bother peeling the tacky clothes from my body before he dumped me onto the shower floor and turned on the water.

"Stolas," I called out. "Plea—fuck! That's cold, you asshole."

He held the nozzle directly over my head, waterboarding me to full alertness. The stench of my soiled clothes, booze, vomit, and sweat intensified as the water finally began to warm then scald my flesh.

Stolas called out over his shoulder, but his words and whoever he'd brought with him were drowned out by my breathing and the pounding of water around us.

He knelt down to my level. "Did you think I was going to allow you to give up? After everything we've been through?"

My head swayed then found purchase on the cool stone wall behind me, but a curtain of my sopping hair fell over my eyes. "You wouldn't understand," I croaked.

My head fell forward and drool slipped from my lips.

A rush of water forced its way into my mouth and up my nose. I pulled my face away and gasped for air. My eyes flew open. Stolas fixed me with a cold glare from only a foot away. He turned the water off and grabbed a fistful of my hair to keep my gaze still.

"I refuse to have you teach me what loss feels like." His anger and disappointment turned his words to poison.

"She . . ."

"I know, brother."

I tried to nod, but his grip and the awkward nature of my equilibrium didn't allow it. My lungs filled with steam, Stolas' cologne, then emptied with a heavy sinking. It wasn't the first time I'd blown my senses with drugs and alcohol, but it was the first time that I had done so with the intent to tempt oblivion. The sweet relief from the vise around my heart would have been a welcome result.

"Help me undress you. I'll help you shower, and after, we will decide if you need to take a trip to the psych hospital."

He pulled at my shirt, the same one I was wearing the last time she touched me. My bare feet held me up long enough for my pants and boxers to be removed. Stolas reached up to the tap and turned the shower back on, but this time to a comfortable temperature. And as if I were a child, he washed my hair and scrubbed my pitiful body.

When he found his job was finished, he was handed two towels from behind him. He smiled to himself but said nothing. Handing one to me, he wrapped the other around my waist.

"Come on. Evie's just finished setting the table."

"You brought her here?" I frantically eyed the empty doorway.

"I needed her close by for her perfection."

"Right."

"You need to eat something to soak up whatever else is left in your system. The cleaners are already working on your bed, though it may be better to get a new mattress and sheets. Yours were torn to shreds as well as being covered in sick."

He leaned against the wall while I dried my hair, neck, chest, and arms.

"I'll just sleep in the guest room for now," I said, my tongue sticking to the roof of my still-too-dry mouth.

"You're coming home with me. My guest room is just as nice as yours."

"I'm assuming I don't have a choice?"

He chuckled, but it held no humor. "It's my house or the hospital. But I'm not leaving you alone either way."

"I am no worse than usual." It was a paper-thin lie.

"You've let that inner darkness take too strong a hold this time, Orobas. This isn't just another depressive episode. I know you can see that too."

I crossed the bathroom to the vanity and evaluated

myself in the mirror. Haggard didn't begin to describe the bags under my eyes or the sunken hollows of my cheeks and temples. Death herself would have confused me for one of her own.

"Falling apart for a woman is weak," I said, slamming a weak fist on the countertop.

"No." Stolas came to my side and stood proud. "Falling apart for the loss of someone so integral to your being is understandable."

"I barely know her," I countered, giving him all the excuses I'd told myself over and over again.

"You would know a piece of your soul if you saw it."

My chest faltered. "She doesn't want me."

"She is scared." He pulled me under his arm. "You have to give her a reason to believe she can be safe with you."

Evelyn's petite frame appeared in the mirror. She hid herself partially behind Stolas, likely heeding a warning he'd given before storming into the disaster zone. He looked over his shoulder at her, and their eyes lit upon contact. My stomach jerked at their bliss and my complete lack thereof.

"Dinner is on the table," she said softly to Stolas.

I'd owned Evelyn's soul since she was a child. I'd watched her grow from a preteen to a young woman who was haunted by her father's sins. The circumstances of our entanglement should have warranted hate toward me, yet she was at my brother's side, caring for my self-inflicted wounds. Perhaps her witnessing my suffering in the arms of my brother was my penance.

"Thank you, lovely." Stalos beamed.

If her doe-like expression was the knife to my gut, his was the rabid boar rooting through my innards for the tenderest meat.

Evelyn left us alone without sparing me a glance while Stolas watched her ass sway through the mirror, obvious obsession brewing in his eyes.

"Let's eat. Then I'll help you pack a bag for our little sober slumber party." He quirked a brow and let the smile overtake his worry.

I nudged his shoulder. "Anything you say, savior."

He winced at the nickname, but that was what he had been for far too long. The burden of being the gaping hole in his armor was the bleeding badge of honor on my chest, and I wore it with grateful fawning.

Like far too many instances before, I followed my brother into the light of another day during which I would fake strength until I found some of my own.

CHAPTER 14

AMBER

12 HOURS AGO

SITRI

Orobas was just here. Did he apologize?

Amber?

Answer or I'm coming to find you then kill my brother.

AMBER

I'm fine. I won't be in for the rest of the week.

SITRI

You're coming back in?

AMBER

Yes. I owe you an explanation, but I just can't right now.

SITRI

You don't owe me anything. I'll see you next week.

I laid my phone on my nightstand, knocking over an empty water bottle and a box of tissues. The ground was littered with the remains of my tearful night. I'd been at war with myself about whether the distress I was violently drowning in was from feelings that were manipulated or real.

I still didn't have an answer.

Oro's words repeated over and over in my head: *"If anyone can, it's you. I need it to be you."*

It could have been me. But no matter how submissive Oro could be, he was still vastly powerful and capable of irreparable damage to my body and soul. That was what I had to keep reminding myself every time I broke down and picked my phone up to call him.

Maybe I was being too harsh in some people's eyes, but in my world, I needed to feel safe to be able to connect with Oro in every way imaginable.

I didn't want to live in fear that a scene would go too far. There were fantasies I had that would mean I'd have all the control with the option to push new boundaries. Orobas had too much power for me to handle, and I had to hold myself responsible for my own limits.

With my midweek time now free, I decided to check in with one of my subs.

AMBER

Missing me yet.

110

SIMONS

You have no idea. I can't bear to wait until Friday. Let me see you tonight and I'll show you how badly you've been missed.

AMBER

What time?

A notification from my bank showed a transfer of five hundred dollars.

SIMONS

Six o'clock. My place. I'll cook.

AMBER

How will you answer the door for me?

SIMONS

Naked except the plug you gave me for my birthday. And maybe an apron if it tickles you in all the right ways.

AMBER

And?

Another notification of an additional five hundred dollars from Simons.

SIMONS

And on my knees. My hands behind my back. Head down.

AMBER

Perfect.

HE REALLY WAS one of my favorite submissives.

Simons' tendencies were malleable to my needs and wants, his bank account seemed never-ending, and his need for my undivided attention fed my soul in more than one way.

The downside to having a multimillionaire as a submissive was that someday, there would come a time when he would have to be seen as settling down or else face the wrath of the public. Only superheroes in black bat masks could get away with being philanthropist playboys forever.

No. Someday, Simons would ask to make our partnership monogamous in exchange for constant comfort and his unwavering obedience. Not a terrible trade-off for most, but I didn't intend to give up my freedom that easily. I enjoyed playing with many subs and teaching the BDSM lifestyle to newcomers to the community. I couldn't do those things if Simons dropped a rock the size of the moon onto my ring finger and called me his missus. Too many eyes would be focused on me, and I hated that sort of attention.

I dragged myself out of bed to get ready for my night. A full-body shower was needed for so many reasons, but most of all to symbolically wash the remaining loss I felt from Oro off my body.

The memories of Oro in my bed would last much longer, but I had to move on. I couldn't let a quick fling destroy me. I didn't become the woman I was by allowing the mistakes of men to affect me. A tryst with a demon was no different. And riding Simons' face after pegging him for hours would be the cure for an ailing heart.

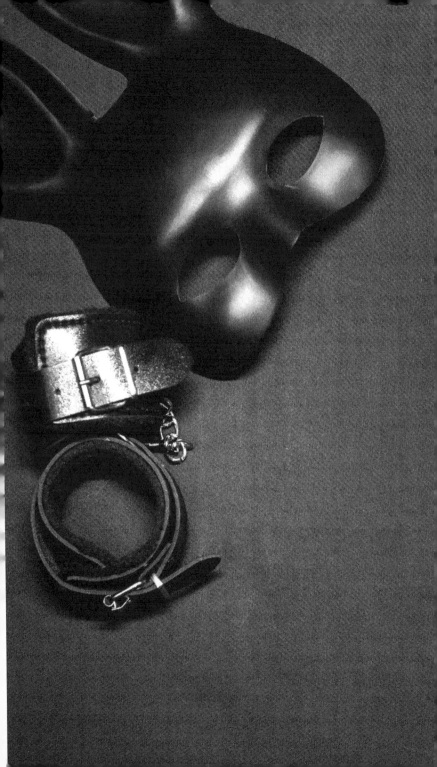

CHAPTER 15
OROBAS

Haniel the Alchemist was a hermit whose skills were far more valuable than those of most others. After the Fall, he'd become essential to all demons because of his God-given talents. His soup and bread were spelled objects for protection. I had a very risky reason for coming to him, but it was the last option I had to plead for a place in Amber's heart.

The instability that Stolas and Evie weaned me through came crashing back with a fury when I found out that Amber had gone out of the country with someone over the weekend. Stolas' living room was in shambles before he tackled me through the void into Hell to cool off.

When the bloodthirst subsided, I returned to Earth with a new goal.

"Are you sure about this, Your Highness?" Haniel's scarred hands wrapped the two gold objects in paper.

"That's none of your business. Your part is finished

and paid for." I looked down at the envelope I'd brought for him.

Season tickets to several basketball games, VIP boxes, and a sizable donation to the animal shelter he frequented. The last one I didn't dare ask any further questions on.

"Then you know the implications and that I have no control over the outcome," he croaked in warning.

"Yes. Yes. I know the fine print well. No returns or refunds." I rolled my eyes and held out my hand for the two small parcels.

"Good luck to you, my liege." He bowed his head. The patches of his burned scalp shined in the fire of his workshop.

"Thank you."

With a sucking pop, I left before he raised his eyes to me. I didn't need another reminder that there was a way out of my plan. I didn't have to put everything on the line for a human, but I intended to spend every one of her waking hours at her whip and flogger until she grew too tired of my company. Then I would be at her side until her soul left the mortal plane and follow her into oblivion for the rest of time.

I only needed her to see past her fear and worry. Show her that I could and would do anything to make her feel safe. The tucked-away gifts were my last chance, and I wouldn't allow myself to formulate a second plan. I needed Amber more than I could put into words, so I'd put them into jewelry.

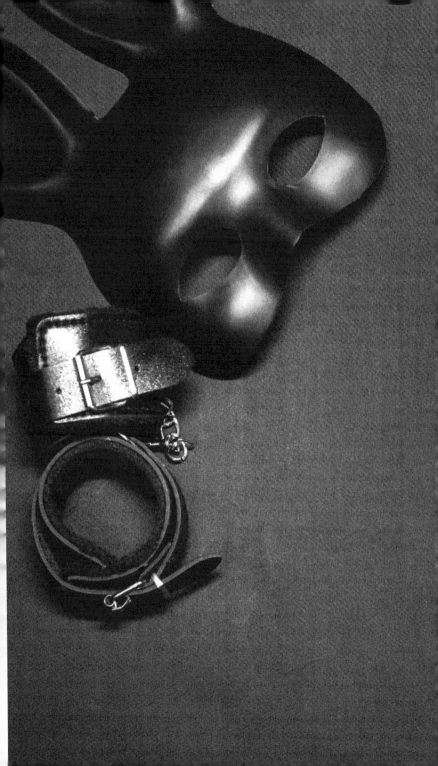

CHAPTER 16
AMBER

P aris was beautiful and exactly what I needed to escape the overwhelming feelings of loss.

At least, that was what I'd told myself for the entire trip.

After I arrived at Simons' house on Wednesday night, he convinced me to hop on his jet the next morning. I didn't bother to pack. He bought me everything I needed once we landed then proceeded to chauffeur me from shop to shop and fill my new luggage with designer clothes, gems, and purses.

I was easily bought with affection and sparkling possessions. Simons had made reservations at the finest restaurants but also at a few sex clubs, where we indulged in our fantasies together and apart. I tried my best not to look over my shoulder for Oro, but to my surprise, he had obeyed my wishes.

A note had been taped to my door when I arrived home:

Amber,

This time apart has been agonizing. I knew I wouldn't be able to rid you from my mind, but the pain I've felt in your absence has been unbearable. Call me pity, for that is all I can ask for. I told you I was not below begging, but in this case, I am groveling in the hope that you will brutalize me with your presence once more before walking away forever.

Meet me at Spago in Beverly Hills on Monday night at 8 o'clock.

I promise this will be my only and last request.

Yours very truly,
Orobas
Prince of Despair

I READ the note over and over, creasing its fold several times in failed symbols of my rejection, only to open it again to admire his handwriting: the delicate, curling tails of his long letters, the soft punctuation. It was as if he hadn't wanted to end what may have been his last words to me.

Prince of Despair.

How very dramatic of him. But that was what this felt

like. Dramatic. He wore his heart on his sleeve so bravely and honestly. He had nothing to lose but me. And I had never imagined he was capable of those types of human emotions.

THE RESTAURANT WAS ALMOST empty for a weekday night. I'd wasted twenty minutes in my car trying to decide whether I was a fool for going or if I'd be even more foolish for leaving and not hearing what he had to say.

Fashionably late was my preferred entry time, but tonight my stomach knotted tighter with each passing minute. When I greeted the host and gave him the name the table was under, the poor man looked as if he'd seen a grisly fate waiting for me. His throat bobbed harshly as his eyes darted to the table where Oro was waiting.

"I don't need an escort." I tapped my fingers on his podium, discreetly laying down a twenty-dollar bill.

Typically, other people's nerves calmed my own. Being the one to inflict pain or pleasure gave me an innate ability to assess a situation before allowing my fight-or-flight reflexes to set in.

Not tonight.

My fingers shook, and the butterflies in my belly raised all sorts of red flags that my feet refused to listen to. Once Oro's eyes met mine, there was no turning back.

He got to his feet when I reached the table. Everything

about him was dipped in otherworldly power. He carried himself with the ease of a man with nothing but time to waste right down to the glint of something sinister behind his eyes, like a predator luring its prey. My showing up was a triumph for him, and it was apparent in his crooked smile.

I greeted him with a pause and nod. "Oro."

He pulled my chair out for me, allowed me to sit, then sat across from me without a word. Perhaps he was choosing them strategically.

"I'm pleasantly surprised you came. Sitri had bet a substantial amount that you wouldn't." His shoulders tensed, like he was bracing for whatever comeback I had.

"Sitri knows me pretty well." I rolled my eyes, realizing that if Sitri had bet against me meeting with Oro, it was probably a sign that I had lost my senses.

"Before you decide whether to take back that choice, I have something for you." He put down a small wrapped bundle and slid it over the white linen-covered table.

"What is it?" My hand hovered over it for a moment.

"A promise."

I quirked my brow at him but unfurled the wrinkled paper until a small silver skeleton key dropped onto the table.

"What—"

"It fits into this." He held up a matching silver lock on a delicate chain.

"Are you asking to be collared?" I looked at the carved inscription on the shaft of the key.

"I'm offering you complete obedience and trust." He scooted his chair closer and laid his hand palm up on the table. "This is more than it seems."

"I have no doubt."

"It has to be your choice, but I want to be yours, Amber. I've never felt more alive than when you are within reach. The insatiable suffering that has gnawed at my soul for thousands of years quiets when you command my attention."

He picked up the charms and got down on his knees beside the table. The few patrons around us turned their gossiping eyes toward us, making my skin heat.

"Oro. We've spent mere hours together—"

"This is not a limited-time offer. I will spend thousands of hours worshiping you if that's what it takes for you to accept this responsibility. Because wielding a prince of Hell is a responsibility, Amber. If the time comes that my power is needed, it will be you who unleashes me unto the Earth once more. Until then, I am only yours to condemn."

Fuck.

"I trust you." The crack of his voice tore at my heart because the implications of my answer applied to more than just the bedroom.

"That's a lot to ask," I finally answered.

"I need it to be you. It's meant to be you. I feel it in every thread of my muscles under my flesh and in the marrow in my bones—you are meant for me."

As graphic as it was, I felt what he did. My nerves had

been twitching and my skin had been itching to feel his touch since I'd arrived. Before I saw him, I sensed him close by and a brutal ache had settled in my chest with the distance I'd kept between us.

"What if I don't want that kind of responsibility? What if it's too much?"

His eyes gleamed up at mine, searching for the crack in my wall. "I am the essence of *too much*. Let my bindings be the separation between you and *too much*."

My eyes fell to the offering in his hands. "I need to think."

"Tell me what your heart says in this moment." He craned his neck for our gazes to meet, the contact sending electricity through me.

"This isn't a matter of my heart, Orobas." He shivered at his own name. "You're asking me to become your keeper, not just your domme. That isn't usually the outcome."

I got to my feet and he followed like I expected him to.

He stepped into me, his face close to mine. "I'm offering you more than any other sub could. Not only physical but complete domination over my soul. This collar won't only symbolize our devotion as partners, but my surrender to your will. And in the thousands of years that I have been collecting souls on this plane, I have never been so close to peace."

My heart pounded against my sternum. The damned thing was trying to detach itself from my body just to beat in his hands.

"Orobas." It was my voice's turn to waver.

He cupped my cheek and brought our foreheads together. "Please take me and never stop saying my name like that."

"Like what?"

"Like your world will shatter if I'm not in it."

Fuck. Fuck. Fuck.

"Okay," I whispered.

"Take it. All of it. Demand everything of me." He offered me the necklace and got back on his knees with his hands joined behind his back.

My mouth watered at how natural it was for him to be in this pose.

He was right. He was made for this, and I was made to put him in his place.

This time, the small crowd around us watched unabashedly. Ignoring the onlookers, I clasped the necklace around his neck then slipped the key into the space between my breasts for safekeeping. It warmed against my skin and picked up my pulse—or had a pulse of its own.

He lifted his chin, and relief washed over his features. His shoulders dropped and he closed his eyes for a moment, as if he were praying, then stood to take me in his arms.

"Can we go somewhere more private?" I said into his shoulder.

"Or you could claim me on top of this table for everyone to see." His playful nature was back. I melted.

"Not now. Eventually, you'll show everyone who owns you, but I want you all to myself tonight."

A wanton groan vibrated his chest, and he hardened against my belly. "Yes, Miss Amber."

"Good boy."

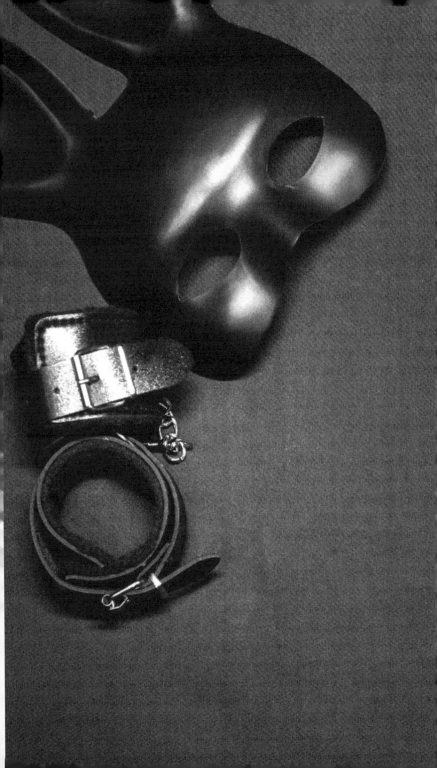

CHAPTER 17
OROBAS

With my demonic powers bound to the two talismans that only Amber could command, I would no longer be able to influence the human race to ravage the world until they burst. I could still take us through the void and into her bedroom, a true blessing.

She gripped my shirt long after her feet were back on solid ground. Her lips trailed kisses over my collarbones then followed her fingers as she unbuttoned my shirt. I groaned when she stopped at my belt.

Her eyes rolled up to mine. "You're going to fuck my throat but you will not come until I say so."

The stern demand filled my cock with greedy blood. It seemed every cell in my veins wanted to be at her lips.

"Yes, Miss Amber." I was out of breath already.

She unbuttoned my pants then drew the zipper down slowly. Each tooth ripped away slower than the last. Her fingers hooked into the waistband of my boxers and moved around to my lower back before she pulled everything over my ass. My cock sprang free with a bounce right at her eye level.

"So hard for me already."

She gripped my shaft and stuck her tongue out to lick a bead of liquid arousal from my throbbing tip. I bit my lip when she began to stroke me, the head of my cock bobbing on and off her juicy lips. This woman knew what she was doing.

I watched intently as she took me into her mouth, hollowed her cheeks, sucking deep, then popped off in quick, shallow motions.

"Oh fuck," I whined. "More."

The words had barely left my throat before she stopped and landed a harsh smack across the head of my dick. I hissed at the shock, but the pain was minor.

"Don't forget your manners, Orobas."

"Please." I pulsed my hips. "I need more, Miss Amber. Please."

"Good." She took all of me deep in her throat, just as she'd promised.

She gripped my waist, and with pressure from her thumbs, she instructed me on how hard to fuck her pretty mouth. Each drag of my hips, I was brought closer to climax and insanity. I knew if I came too soon—and without permission—she would punish me in whatever fashion she desired. But more than anything, I wanted to please her and make her proud of my restraint.

I felt her throat constricting around me as I pushed farther. She used one hand to roughly cup my balls, and the other to dig her nails into my abdomen, then she dragged them down. The dark red lines sent hot flames to my core. My knees buckled at the intense pleasure.

"Miss Amber?"

She knew what I was asking with such desperation in my voice. Without missing a single thrust, she shook her head and hummed something that felt like "no."

"Please," I begged. "I need to come."

I whimpered and tried to slow my rhythm, but her hands took hold of my hips and manipulated them to keep pace.

"*Fuck.*" The word was long and drawn out.

She shook her head again then sucked me harder.

"Please, let me come," I repeated over and over.

The sound of my own pathetic voice put me in a trance once again. Begging this woman to allow me to abide by my body's natural urges only to be denied felt like life and death. She was the master of my orgasms, and they would only comply with her darkest wishes.

I held myself up against the nearest bit of furniture, but the dresser was not enough to keep me from slumping onto my knees. Her mouth took over as I leaned back with my hands digging into the carpet. My back arched as another stunted wave of pleasure washed over me. I clenched my thighs and stomach.

One of her hands held the base of my cock, while the other braced her weight on my stomach. I focused on the tension of her back, ass, and arm, but her head rapidly bobbed up and down on my cock.

I let out one last cursed moan, and she took her mouth away and began feverishly pumping me.

"You want to come?" Her bruised vocal cords strained against the question.

"I need to come, Miss Amber." I kicked my head back and let out another frustrated moan.

"Have you earned it?"

"Yes," I breathed.

"I can't hear you."

"Yes. Yes. Yes."

My throbbing cock ached and my balls had tightened to the point of pain. I would die if I couldn't come soon.

Her hands stopped. "Show me you deserve to come."

My head shot up to find her pulling her dress up and over her head, revealing her bare, dripping pussy. She mounted me, her beautiful tits inches from my greedy mouth. I wrapped an arm around her waist and used her frame to pump my cock. Her cunt squeezed me while my swollen head slammed up into her.

I sucked one of her nipples and flicked my tongue over the hard pebble. She let out a moan and gripped the back of my head to hold me there. Her body was flush against mine as our sweat mingled on our hot, slick skin.

"Come for me, Orobas," she demanded. "Fuck me and fill my pussy with cum."

No answer was needed.

I took us down to the floor with her back on the carpet. I pounded into her until I burst and my cum gushed with the waves of my orgasm until I was spent.

Her heavy breaths mimicked mine, but I knew she

hadn't had her fill. I withdrew but replaced my cock with three fingers to spread her wide for me. My mouth trailed down her neck, my tongue lapping up the salt of her flesh while I made my way to her perfect, made-for-me cunt. She was glistening with my release, her clit swollen from excitement. I domed my mouth over it and flicked my tongue in quick circles as my fingers pumped inside of her.

"I need to make you come," I said into her soft folds. "I need it more than I need to breathe."

"Make me come." She fisted my hair and bucked against my face.

I grunted and whined as my fingers and tongue fucked her senseless. Every pulse of pleasure she felt was commanded. Her first orgasm shook her legs, but the second and third released gushes of ambrosia that I drank like a man dying of thirst. I would never get enough of what she allowed me to have. If it meant begging on my knees in every pit of fiery Hell, I would gladly do it just to hear her breathlessly moan my name.

She owned me. And I would spend the rest of time earning that title.

CHAPTER 18
AMBER

When I walked into The Deacon on Wednesday evening, Ezequiel was perched atop of the bar with a beautiful woman sitting on a stool between his legs. Her elbows were propped on his thighs, and she looked up at him as if he'd hung every star in the galaxy just for her. As far as I knew, he had.

"You came back?" Sitri called across the dance floor. He looked like he had just come down the stairs from his office.

"I told you that I would. You know I don't break promises." I placed my hands on my cocked hips.

"Well, after an encounter with Orobas, I wasn't sure if you'd been scared off for good." He stopped several steps away and looked me over as if assessing me for injuries.

"He isn't so terrible."

Sitri's brows flew up.

"Oh fuck, he's gotten to you, hasn't he?" Ezequiel said behind me, homing in on the conversation.

"I sure have."

As if saying his name with kindness had summoned him, Orobas sauntered through the front door, looking like walking sex. His arrogance wasn't unwarranted, but it still took me by surprise.

I looked from Orobas to Ezequiel, whose face lit with a menacing smile. Ezequiel's eyes panned over to Sitri and mine followed. Sitri's heated glare could have sparked a wildfire.

Orobas pressed a hand to my lower back, and his lips brushed the shell of my ear. "You may want to take this moment as the one to claim me in front of everyone present or else you'll be picking pieces of my body up to deposit into a dumpster."

I cleared my throat and stepped in front of Orobas. Sitri's lethal stare flicked down to the key dangling from the chain on my chest.

"He did not force me, Sitri. I chose him." I tried to sound confident, but there were still bits of our arrangement that Orobas could have easily initiated.

"Amber—"

"He's given me plenty of reasons to trust him, and until he breaks that trust, Sitri, I'm not worried." I reached a hand behind me to grip Orobas' shirt and pull him closer.

Orobas took the cue and wrapped an arm around my middle. His touch was stabilizing, but more importantly, it eased Sitri's anger.

Sitri gave us another head-to-toe glance, and then his shoulders relaxed. "All right, I supposed this calls for a drink before the club opens."

He motioned at Ezequiel and the mysterious woman, who was now standing. Ezequiel lifted himself up like an acrobat and swung himself backward behind the bar, sticking his landing and receiving a round of applause from his admirer.

"Show off," Orobas called, adding pressure to his hold on me in the direction of the stools.

He waited for me to accept the invitation before we joined the others.

"What can we make for you?" Ezequiel didn't take his eyes off me but held his hand up in the direction of the woman at his side.

"Dirty martini. Two olives," I answered, sitting at the bar next to Orobas, who was watching the new bartender closely.

There was something familiar about her, like I'd been waiting to meet an old friend after a long time apart. She effortlessly poured liquor from the glass bottles into the shaker then strained the cloudy liquid into the chilled martini glass in front of me.

Sitri came to sit on my other side. He turned so his knees framed my body and he could see everyone without having to crane his neck. "Does this mean I can finally rent out the BDSM room to the furries?"

I shot him a warning look. "Don't you dare."

"I love it when you're demanding." His flirtatious grin spread warmth through my belly.

I wrinkled my nose at him and took a sip of my drink. It wasn't as good as Sitri's, but it was a decent attempt.

"You're delightfully better at making a whiskey sour than the angel is." The sultry dip in Orobas' voice drew my attention back to him and the new bartender. He was testing a boundary, I knew, but the bratty behavior coiled in my belly nonetheless.

The glare I gave him was likely boring holes into the side of his head.

"Ezequiel is a good teacher," she replied and poured three fingers of dark liquor into a glass for Sitri. "Mixing the spicy and sweet liquids together is new to me, but I'm learning quickly."

"Amber, this is Dabria," Sitri proclaimed.

"It's nice to meet you." Dabria smiled, and warmth spread through me.

"You're not human, are you?" The words slipped from my lips too high-pitched.

She giggled, and her intoxicating personality drew me in and erased the moment of jealousy. Her brown eyes glinted in the overhead light. She was wearing a gorgeous dress that plunged to accentuate her large chest. The shimmery black material hugged her curvy middle and stretched over her thick hips before ending at her upper thigh.

She was obviously gorgeous, but there was a sweetness to her smile. Except when she looked at Sitri or Ezequiel. They brought a flush to her cheeks. Another bubble of jealousy grew in my chest when I noticed the reactions only they brought out of her. Suddenly, I wanted to be the only one in the club with her and see what else made her blush like that.

Was I in love with this woman? Maybe she was some sort of enchantress.

"No." She looked to each man for permission. "I'm a Reaper."

Ice surged through my veins and I recoiled.

She reached out her free hand. "Don't worry, I can't hurt you."

"Our little Reaper can't harm you unless it's your time to die," Sitri practically purred as he gave Dabria a look that could melt the polar ice caps.

"That's good to know." I shivered.

When I looked at Orobas, he was staring at me as if I were made of glass. He dropped his gaze to the top of his thigh where his palm was expectantly waiting. I took it and squeezed.

"Is this too . . . much?" He quirked a brow.

I shook my head. "Just another day in L.A."

He smirked then looked at Sitri. "Stolas and I will be occupying our booth upstairs tonight."

"Naturally," Sitri answered without any question.

"I have to set up the rooms." I dismounted my stool and started walking to the hidden rooms at the back of the club. "The theme is going to be a bit messy tonight."

"I wouldn't expect anything else," he replied with a regal wave of his hand.

I would be exhausted by the end of the night. Orobas being at the club didn't change my previous commitments. While my subs rarely requested to be shared or to share an experience, they each demanded my attention in ways that satisfied them. Allen and Simons' needs were just as important to me as my own or Orobas'. Taking on another sub hadn't been on my mind before Orobas walked into my life, but he fit in like a missing piece of my soul.

Allen had been looking forward to the night's events all week. Since he'd missed his last appointment, we were both excited for the scene. The room was set with my usual whips, floggers, and strap-ons, but also included wax, oil, and a massage table. His acts of service were rewarded with the marks of my crop.

The second room was equipped similarly, but I set out the rubber mat, towels, and a tarp. The couple booked for this room were into much wetter play. They had joined the weekly meetups months ago and often brought newcomers to join them. My role would be to introduce the concept and safety practices and be available if there were any jitters.

In the last room, Veronica was bringing her newest sub. They'd met during an orgy in this very room several months back but only recently turned their random hookups into a more solid relationship. I cleaned the Saint Andrew's cross and cuffs and brought out the electrodes to ensure everything was working correctly. Since Allen would be coming a bit later, I would be available for my patrons before satisfying my own sub.

Watching Veronica work gave me a sense of pride but also turned me on. She'd blossomed in her new role and executed the punishments and rewards with grace and confidence. She was a soft domme, but there were certain kinks that easily flipped the switch to pleasure domme.

When I was finally finished for the night, Orobas was waiting at the door. Allen was still collecting himself after being flogged and fucked to within an inch of his life in our room. I was on my way to grab a drink to allow him space to rest before I checked on him.

"How was your night?" Orobas tipped his head in the direction of the secret doors.

"Gratifying," I said simply. "Are you feeling neglected?"

"Not at all." He shrugged. "I just wanted to be sure you were escorted home like the queen you are."

"I need another half hour."

"Then I'll wait."

I perked a brow at him.

"If I seemed pathetic enough, I was hoping you'd allow me to bathe you then kneel at your bedside until I could be of use."

Those words went straight to my clit. "You can beg at the bar."

I laced my fingers with his and led the way.

OROBAS

S tolas grunted dramatically as he hauled another box of Amber's things from the moving truck to bring into my house. It didn't take much convincing on my part to get her to agree to move in with me. I had plenty of room and was spending every waking moment I could in her presence. Stolas had too often hinted that my workload at the firm was becoming too lax due to my preoccupation. He was right. My quarterly earnings had taken a nosedive along with my soul count. Two things I'd always prided myself on no longer satisfied my needs. But I still had duties to my crown and to Hell to fulfill if I didn't want to incur the wrath of Lucifer or, worse, Evie.

Evelyn had moved into Stolas' house quite quickly after her father had withdrawn his name from the presidential race and resigned his position as governor. It was rather tempting to poke at his wounds, but I was scolded in three directions when I vocalized the impulse.

"You couldn't get the job done the first time," Stolas had told me. "I don't trust you to fuck with that man's mind without creating a problem for me. Evie has been through enough trauma at your hands."

He wasn't wrong.

What he didn't know was that the binding of my abilities meant that I had to use much more of my demonic energy to perform any sort of deal. My silver tongue was doing more than pleasuring my domme daily. Talking wealthy men into doing despicable things for more money wasn't difficult, but I had to bring Stolas in during larger dealings for his influence and deal-sealing abilities.

There would be a time when I would be offered the opportunity to regain my potent power, but the more Amber's essence seeped into the slivers of my being, the more certain I was that I would no longer reside on Earth when her Reaper came to call. My soul was meant to be bound to her for eternity in any way possible. Following her into oblivion would be as easy a decision to make as it had been to cohabitate.

"Orobas," her siren voice called from the upstairs balcony, "do you need encouragement to finish?"

My lips twitched at her innuendo and the roll of Stolas' eyes as he came back to the truck with a giggling Evie in tow.

"Yes, Miss Amber. Always."

THE END

Ridden hard and put away dirty Martini

3 oz Ciroc Ten Vodka

.5 oz Dry Vermouth

Dash of olive brine

Shaken with Ice

Garnish with three olives

ACKNOWLEDGMENTS

I want to give the highest praise to Rae (@seeraeread) and Ash (@ashleymichelelx) for not only helping me understand the world of kink, but guiding me through the representation of the community.

I also want to give the biggest hug to Nemmy for inspiring one of my most fun spicy scenes yet!

Thank you to my readers for coming along on this journey of sin.

Made in the USA
Columbia, SC
28 September 2024